Rendez~~vous with~~ destiny

A sudden flash of light ahead drew her up short. She narrowed her eyes and squinted through the gloom. There it was again, the proverbial light at the end of the tunnel. Disappointment made her shoulders sag. The tunnel must be far more recent than she had thought, if it contained a form of lighting.

Either that or it had been discovered already and was being used for some purpose, perhaps as a storage area for workers servicing the intricate conduits of power lines, water pipes and so on that honeycombed the city's subsurface.

Except that she had seen no indication of any such use other than the light itself, which she suddenly realized was coming from a flashlight much like her own. A light that was suddenly clicked off.

Someone else was in the tunnel.

Dear Reader,

When two people fall in love, the world is suddenly new and exciting, and it's that same excitement we bring to you in Silhouette Intimate Moments. These are stories with scope, with grandeur. These characters lead the lives we all dream of, and everything they do reflects the wonder of being in love.

Longer and more sensuous than most romances, Silhouette Intimate Moments novels take you away from everyday life and let you share the magic of love. Adventure, glamour, drama, even suspense—these are the passwords that let you into a world where love has a power beyond the ordinary, where the best authors in the field today create stories of love and commitment that will stay with you always.

In coming months look for novels by your favorite authors: Maura Seger, Parris Afton Bonds, Elizabeth Lowell and Erin St. Claire, to name just a few. And whenever you buy books, look for all the Silhouette Intimate Moments, love stories *for* today's women *by* today's women.

Leslie J. Wainger
Senior Editor
Silhouette Books

IMRL-7/85

Maura Seger
Quest of the Eagle

Silhouette Intimate Moments

Published by Silhouette Books New York

America's Publisher of Contemporary Romance

SILHOUETTE BOOKS
300 East 42nd St., New York, N.Y. 10017

ISBN: 0-373-07149-3

First Silhouette Books printing July 1986

America's Publisher of Contemporary Romance

Printed in the U.S.A.

Books by Maura Seger

Silhouette Special Edition

A Gift Beyond Price #135

Silhouette Intimate Moments

Silver Zephyr #61
Golden Chimera #96
Comes a Stranger #108
Shadows of the Heart #137
Quest of the Eagle #149

Silhouette Desire

Cajun Summer #282

MAURA SEGER

was prompted by her love of books and vivid imagination to decide, at age twelve, to be a writer. Twenty years later, her first book was published. So much, she says, for overnight success! Now each book is an adventure, filled with fascinating people who always surprise her.

Chapter 1

She should have gone home.

After five P.M. on a summer Friday was no time to be prowling through the company archives trying to locate an obscure piece of information a partner claimed he absolutely had to have over the weekend.

Two levels above her, on the ground floor of the Cabot Brothers Bank, Wall Street was empty. Stray bits of newspaper blew around lamp posts, propelled by the hot breeze that had seared the city for a week. Anyone with any sense was on his way to the Hamptons.

Except Mollie Fletcher. She opened another file drawer, releasing a shower of dust, and sneezed again. Patting her reddened nose with a wilted tissue, she muttered under her breath.

If good jobs as company librarians weren't so hard to find, she might give some thought to moving on. The problem was that Cabot Brothers, the oldest privately owned bank in the United States, not only paid better than anyone else but also provided her with an exciting, often challenging job.

Her present assignment, however, was neither. There was nothing remotely exciting or challenging about searching through decades-old files for a report that might well never have existed.

"All this stuff should have been microfiched years ago," Mollie grumbled. "Or better yet, burned." She brushed aside a stray lock of her auburn hair. Generally, she kept it pulled back in a neat chignon, but toward the end of the day it tended to get untidy, particularly when the heat and humidity made it curl.

The chignon—a less elegant name for it would have been a bun—was a private Mollie joke. By wearing her hair that way, she knew she was paying tribute to the stereotype of the old-maidish librarian, as she also did with her sensible shoes and generally simple clothes. But beyond that, the stereotype most definitely did not apply, and the contrast often had humorous results.

Mollie had—as her mother tactfully put it—blossomed early. By the time she was thirteen, her training bras had been relegated to the trash-bin, and she was becoming adept at ignoring the open-mouthed stares of awed boys in the school yard. Her breasts were by no means excessively large, but they appeared bigger than they were by virtue of an exceptionally small waist, which gave way in turn to gently rounded hips and spectacularly long, tapered legs.

Since she also had delicate oval features, large green eyes, and thick, wavy auburn hair, it was no wonder that on the rare occasions when she deliberately played up her appearance, it made grown men stop dead in their tracks.

As nearly as anyone in the family could figure out, she was a throwback to her great-great-Aunt Amelia, a famous—or infamous, depending on your point of view—courtesan of the Gilded Age. Amelia had reigned supreme among the elite of Europe and the Americas for almost two decades. She had counted among her lovers a crown prince, three dukes, four counts, innumerable barons, and a flock of mere millionaires.

Until her retirement in 1900—which she had announced while drinking champagne in Delmonico's Restaurant precisely at the stroke of 12:00 a.m. as the new century was born—she had raised more feminine eyebrows and caused more fans to flutter in agitation than almost any other woman who had ever lived. Amelia would not have appreciated the "almost." She never willingly took second place to anyone.

Mollie's resemblance to the legendary Amelia was both a blessing and a curse. While it was quite pleasant sometimes to be able to "knock 'em dead," as her brother William insisted on putting it, she knew that she did not in any way share her ancestress's disregard of more conventional morality.

It was the irony of Mollie's life that she who had grown up during the sexual revolution was far less liberated in this regard than a woman who had been born more than a century before.

Reluctantly, she pulled her thoughts back from great-great-Aunt Amelia and concentrated instead on the yellowed pages of correspondence bearing long-forgotten names, dealing with long-forgotten matters.

Another sneeze was starting when she abruptly flinched. Her finger had caught the sharp edge of a piece of paper, resulting in one of those nasty little cuts that were an occupational hazard.

"Ouch." Reflexively, she licked the wound, tasting the iron tang of her blood. When she looked at the finger again, it was still bleeding. A soft sigh of impatience escaped her as she closed the file drawer and looked around for a paper towel or anything else she could use to staunch the flow.

The bank's archives were kept in a low-ceilinged sub-basement dimly lit by pale yellow globes from some long-ago era. Rumor had it that the present building had been raised over a much older structure, and Mollie believed it.

The floor beneath her feet was stone, not poured concrete, but honest granite of the type that made up most of Manhattan Island. In recent years, few people had walked on it, but at some earlier time it must have seen heavy use, for it was worn down in places.

Acoustic tiles with built-in sprinklers covered the original ceiling, but once she had come down to the archives when workmen had removed a section of the tiles. Above them had been a wooden plank ceiling crisscrossed by sturdy beams blackened with age.

The air in the sub-basement invariably smelled damp and musty, the odor she associated with things that had existed for a long time and had soaked up the essence of time passing. There was also a faint, lingering suggestion of smokiness, which she could not fully explain, but which might have come from fireplaces long sealed over.

Mollie was something of a student of early New York history. On her days off, she liked to roam around the older parts of the city, imagining what it had been like when only a few thousand people lived perched on the tip of an island that was largely unsettled before it had become the hub of the world.

She took secret pleasure in studying a block of steel-and-glass skyscrapers, knowing that where they stood had once been the farm of a sturdy Dutchman, or wandering through a park imagining the marsh it had once been and the duck hunters who had gathered there with flint and musket.

She knew the streets beneath which buried rivers and canals still ran, the places where hills, valleys and coves had been reshaped to fit the needs of men, the secret contours of a world invisible to the less-imaginative eye, but vividly real to her.

Truth be told, she did not always like what New York had become, but she stayed because the sense of being part of something linking both past and future fascinated her. The city gave the impression of being relentlessly anchored to the present, but she knew that for what it was—a convenient mask worn to fool the uninitiated.

She gave up looking for something to put on her finger and went in search of the utility closet, which she knew was regularly left unlocked because so few people ever ventured into the sub-basement. A yank on the string connected to a bare bulb overhead revealed a good-sized space large enough for her to walk into. The closet was lined with shelves holding various useful items, except along the far wall, where they had been removed and stacked neatly on the floor.

She noted this absently as she found a roll of paper towels, opened them, and applied a sheet to her finger. After a few moments the bleeding stopped, and she was able to take closer stock of her surroundings.

There was something odd about the back wall; it seemed...loose. When she looked at it more carefully, she noticed that the plasterboard appeared to have been moved aside, then put back in place, but not completely.

Touching it lightly, she confirmed that it was only set against another, hidden wall, not actually attached to it. Curiosity darted through her. Her fascination with the old building and the desire to know more about it prompted her to gently ease the plaster-board away and looked behind it.

She could see nothing except a dark wall apparently made of wood. Telling herself that she was being silly, she nonetheless lifted the false wall and carefully set it aside.

A soft gasp escaped her. Instead of the old but otherwise nondescript wall she had expected to find, she discovered instead an oak door studded with brass fittings that were pitted by age.

Doors usually led to other places, but she could not imagine that this one still did. Once, long ago, it might have guarded a storage room of some sort, or perhaps even led out onto a long-buried street.

No, that last part was wrong. Even with all the changes that had occurred, the streets in lower Manhattan were where they had always been; they even continued to bear their original names. Whatever the building had once been, it had fronted on Wall Street, with its entrance behind her.

Gingerly, she tried the latch. It felt very stiff, but lifted as she pressed down on the handle. The door opened toward her. She pulled on it, hearing the hinges creak.

Curious though she was, she half hoped to find only another wall on the other side of the door, which would put an end to her exploring. There was work to be done if she ever hoped to get out of here; she had no time to mess around with dead ends.

Except that it wasn't. Even the dim light in the closet was enough to show her that beyond the door was a flight of stone steps leading downward into darkness. A basement, that's what must be down there. The basement of the original building. Over the centuries, the ground level in lower Manhattan had risen considerably as human occupation deposited successive layers of debris, so that what had once been a basement only a few feet below ground level was now deeply buried.

Until recently little thought had been given to the archaeological treasures being lost. It was possible that no one had ventured into the basement in a century or more. Her heart beat more quickly at that thought.

The chance to see a part of the old city untouched by modern hands thrilled her. Even as she knew that the odds of finding anything more than a fragment of glass or a sliver of wood were extremely remote, she couldn't resist the urge to try.

But first she would need more light. The yellow lamps in the ceiling of the sub-basement were so notoriously inadequate that she had brought a high-powered flashlight with her, but had left it in her shoulder bag near where she had been working. Going back for it took only a few minutes, but increased her impatience to see what the basement might hold.

The flashlight beam revealed that the stone steps were stained with mold, reminding her that the building lay between two rivers. As she descended carefully, she could feel the dampness seeping through the thin cotton blouse and skirt she had put on that morning in deference to the heat. Not even the thin sweater she had pulled from her desk drawer before venturing into the sub-basement could keep her from feeling chilled.

She shone the light ahead of her, trying to make out the dimensions of the basement. If, as she suspected given the building's location, it had once served a warehouse or tavern, it shouldn't be particularly large. Still, she was struck by its narrowness, until she realized that she could make out only three walls; the expected fourth did not exist.

She had not entered a basement, as she had thought, but a passage leading to an unknown destination. Common sense told her to turn back. It was the height of folly to explore such a place alone. Aside from the risk of cave-ins, there were bound to be rats, spiders and all manner of other unpleasant inhabitants. Besides, while interesting items might have been stored in a basement, the chance of finding anything of archaeological value in a tunnel was remote.

Still, there was the question of why anyone would go to all the effort of constructing an underground passage. Presumably to do something without being seen. That opened up all sorts of interesting possibilities. She knew that during certain times in New York's history, smuggling had been at least as commonplace as legitimate trade.

There were still rumors of tunnels beneath the city, some of which had been turned into huge vaults to store particularly important items far below the city's surface. One story even had it that billions of dollars worth of gold was hidden in such a tunnel somewhere in the financial district.

She smiled wryly. It was a cinch that she had not stumbled on that particular tunnel, if it even existed. There was no indication that anyone had used this dank passageway in a very long time indeed. Water trickled down the walls, pooling in places on the dirt floor. She stepped gingerly over the stagnant puddles, trying not to cringe at a rustling sound nearby.

A rat, disturbed by her presence, peered at her with gleaming yellow eyes. Mollie swallowed and moved on. She knew, from her days living on a farm in New Hampshire, that rats would not attack in the presence of light; at least, nice rural rats wouldn't. She could only hope that the city breed was the same.

The tunnel had to end soon, she reasoned. With all the construction that had gone on in New York, it must have been at least partially filled in long ago. Besides, if she was right about it having once been used by smugglers, it would have reached no further than the original shoreline, now several blocks distant from the river.

A sudden flash of light ahead drew her up short. She narrowed her eyes and squinted through the gloom. There it was again, the proverbial light at the end of the tunnel. Disappointment made her shoulders sag. The tunnel must be far more recent than she had thought if it contained some form of lighting.

Either that or it had been discovered after all and was being used for some purpose, perhaps as a storage area for workers servicing the intricate conduits of power lines, water pipes and such that honeycombed the city's subsurface.

She had seen no indication of any such use other than the light itself, which, she realized as she watched, was coming from a flashlight much like her own. A light that was suddenly clicked off.

Someone else was in the tunnel.

Mollie had always prided herself on her good sense. It had caused her to choose a profession that afforded her both enjoyment and a roof over her head, prevented her from becoming involved with several men who would inevitably have broken her heart, and all in all was responsible for what she considered a very nice life.

What it was telling her right then was to run as quickly as her sensible low-heeled shoes would take her. She was very tempted to obey, except that she seemed unaccountably frozen in place. The combination of darkness, isolation, peculiar noises, and an abrupt sense of her own vulnerability, kept both her brain and her body from functioning as they would have normally.

Instead of retreating, she remained where she was, her ears straining for any sound that might reveal the whereabouts of the other person. When none came, she tried to believe that she had only imagined the light. That didn't work.

Mollie had an excellent imagination when she chose to use it, but it did not mislead her. The light had been there; now it was not. Either there was another way to enter and exit the tunnel, or whoever else was there didn't want to be seen.

No great insight was needed to realize that if someone else wanted his presence kept secret from her, he might not take well to suddenly discovering her there. Belatedly, she clicked off her own flashlight and pressed herself back against the wall. Cool moisture seeped through her blouse as she waited, barely breathing.

The footsteps, when she first heard them, were so faint that several moments passed before she realized what they meant. By the time she did and tried to meld herself even more firmly into the wall, the man was almost upon her.

She knew it was a man because even in the darkness the gender of the tall, muscular shape was unmistakable. He moved gracefully, as though accustomed to doing without light. Her own eyes had adjusted to the dimness by then, and she caught a glimpse of his profile as he passed, a strong chin and hawklike nose beneath thick, dark hair.

Not until she heard him go up the stairs and through the door did she allow herself to breath again. Even then she waited several more minutes to give him time to get completely away. Later she might regret not knowing who else had shared her interest in the tunnel, but just then she had no thought except eluding him.

When she was sure it was safe, she moved away from the wall. Not trusting herself to find her way as easily as the man had, she turned her flashlight back on, but kept it cupped in the palm of her hand so that only a thin beam showed.

Going as quickly as she dared, she retraced her steps toward the stairs. They were directly in front of her, with the door in sight, when a steely arm abruptly wrapped around her throat, pressing her back against a rock-hard form, and the breath was forced from her with merciless ease.

The last things Mollie remembered were the whirling of colored lights in front of her eyes, the rush of blood in her ears, and the thought that her family would never know how she had died.

Chapter 2

Eagle stared down at the woman in his arms. She was deeply unconscious, as he had intended when he pressed on her windpipe while simultaneously cutting off the flow of blood through the carotid artery in her throat.

Precise knowledge—and experience—were needed to effect such a maneuver without bringing about the death of the victim. That he had not intended, at least not before he could question her.

The problem was that she didn't look like a terrorist. But then, who did? The popular image fostered by the mass media of the terrorist as a wild-eyed degenerate was sadly mistaken. All too many of them blended perfectly with the mass of ordinary people who were more likely than not their next victim.

When he had realized that he was not alone in the tunnel, his first thought had been that he had walked into a trap. The letter from the terrorist group that had resulted in his present assignment had made claims so outrageous that Eagle himself had refused to believe them, until he sat down with a man from the Library of Congress and heard for himself that they might be true.

Might. That was the rub. He could be on a wild goose chase, in which case the young lady in his arms was a complete innocent. On the other hand, she might be a very clever operative whose luck had simply run out.

Luck. That was what it so often came down to in his world. A moment's hesitation could cost a man his life before he even knew what had happened to him.

A man or a woman. He laid her down carefully, observing her in the narrow beam of light from the flashlight he pulled from beneath his black jacket.

She looked very pale, understandably, given what he had done to her. His gaze drifted to her breasts, which rose and fell steadily. The tightening of his loins made him frown. He couldn't afford responses like that no matter how natural they might be.

Fingers touched to her throat confirmed that her pulse was regular. She'd be coming around soon. Before she did so, he wanted to make sure she wasn't carrying any weapons. His hands moved over her with deliberation, spanning her breasts, her small waist and rounded hips, her slender thighs and long legs.

Damn, but she was beautiful beneath the plain clothes she wore. Whoever, whatever, she was, she came dangerously close to making him forget the cardinal rules on which his very life depended: take nothing for granted, suspect everyone, and, above all, allow no distractions.

The one time he'd forgotten those rules he'd come away with the scar that ran from his forehead down his left cheek, barely missing his eye, and he counted himself fortunate to have escaped so lightly.

Mollie moaned softly, her thick lashes fluttering against her pale cheeks. Eagle sat back on his haunches and watched her. The fact that she carried no weapons didn't convince him one way or the other about her identity. He'd known plenty of extremely efficient killers who never carried so much as a length of rope. Their bodies were their weapons.

He smiled slightly, thinking that the lovely form before him could be a potent weapon under certain circumstances. He caught himself wondering what she was like in bed, and his features tightened grimly.

That was what Mollie saw when she opened her eyes. The man staring at her looked like a statue carved from granite, completely unyielding. There was no flicker of humanity in his hooded eyes, or in the set of his finely drawn mouth. The scar that ran across his left cheek added the final touch to a sinister appearance.

She swallowed hard and tried to sit up. A rough hand on her shoulder pushed her back. "Don't move until I say you can."

Even dazed as she was, Mollie had too much sense to think of disobeying him. She concentrated all her strength on trying to understand what was happening to her as she murmured, "Wh-who . . . who are you?"

The man shrugged. "That doesn't matter. What are you doing down here?"

She shook her head, trying to clear it. Surely a rapist or robber wouldn't bother asking questions. "Exploring . . . I found the door."

"And you decided it would be nice to see where it led?" He sneered at her openly, not bothering to make any secret of his disbelief. "You expect me to believe that you chose to enter a dark tunnel by yourself with nothing but a flashlight simply because you thought it would be fun?"

"Believe what you want," Mollie said stiffly. "Whatever my reason for coming down here, you had no right to do what you did."

She touched her throat tentatively as the full impact of what had happened began to sink in. "Knocking me unconscious, bringing me back down here . . . I've got a good mind to go to the police."

No sooner were the words out than she regretted them. The last thing she wanted to do was make this rough-and-ready man feel threatened by her. Not, apparently, that she could. His laughter was deep and rich, the only really nice thing she had noticed about him so far, except that it was directed against her.

"Police?" he said. "That's cute. Either you've got solid steel nerves or..."

"Or what?" she asked, half suspecting she would regret his answer.

"Or you're what you seem to be, except that I still don't buy the idea that you came down here on your own."

"Why else would I? This tunnel must have been abandoned at least a hundred years ago." How she prayed that was true. If it were still in use, she might have stumbled across far more than she could hope to handle.

Warily, she tried to sit up again and was relieved when this time he didn't stop her. But his unrelenting gaze and the taut readiness she sensed in the big body so near her own told her that should she go an inch further than he was inclined to allow, he would stop her instantly.

"My name is Mollie Fletcher," she said quietly, forcing herself to meet his gaze. "I'm a librarian with Cabot Brothers, the bank that owns the building above us. I was working late in the sub-basement and cut myself."

She held up her finger. "I went to get a paper towel from the utility closet and noticed that the back wall was loose. That's how I found the door and came down here."

Eagle looked from the thin red line on her finger to her slightly flushed face. She was afraid of him, but doing a good job of hiding it. He had to admire that. "Didn't it occur to you that that it might be dangerous to come down here?"

"Not at first," she admitted ruefully. "You see, I'm very interested in local history, and the chance to explore someplace really old was too good to pass up."

He smiled despite himself. "Do you still feel that way?"

"No," she admitted. "How can I, after being scared out of my wits?"

"You don't look scared." Actually she did, a little. Her green eyes were unusually large, and her full mouth trembled slightly, all of which only added to her undeniable appeal. He had to clench his fists to keep from reaching out for her, which undoubtedly would only have frightened her more.

"Well, Mollie Fletcher," he said at length, "you picked a bad day to go exploring. Now the question is, what am I going to do with you?"

"Forget you ever saw me?" she suggested. "I'd be willing to do the same for you." Actually, she knew she could never do anything of the kind; even if she told no one about him, he would remain forever imprinted on her mind.

"It's not that simple." He stood up, dusting off his hands before holding one out to her. "Get up. I want to make sure you're all right."

She did as he said, gingerly, telling herself that he wouldn't be concerned about her well-being if he meant her any further harm. The touch of his hand on hers was warm and dry. She could feel the strength in his arms as he effortlessly hoisted her to her feet and studied her critically.

"How are you feeling?"

"Fine," she said, even though she was a little dizzy. She didn't want to give him any excuse for making her stay in the tunnel a moment longer than she could avoid.

Her small effort at duplicity failed completely. He knew she was still feeling the effects of what he had done, and experienced a brief flash of regret. That faded as he reminded himself that she had yet to prove her identity.

"We're going back upstairs," he told her. "You're going to show me where you work."

"But there won't be anyone there," she protested unthinkingly, realizing only after the fact that he would consider that a plus.

"And," he went on relentlessly as he took her elbow and steered her toward the steps, "let's also hope you've got convincing identification."

"Just who do you think you are?" Mollie demanded, trying unsuccessfully to free herself from his hold. "You've got no right to make me prove anything."

"Maybe not, but you'll do it anyway." He pushed open the heavy wooden door at the top of the steps and walked through it, all without releasing her.

Mollie blinked in the light of the supply closet. She glanced at the tall, somber-faced man, hoping that being able to see him better might give her some clue as to his identity and purpose. But all she was able to determine was that he was every bit as ruthless looking as she had already surmised.

Dressed in a black windbreaker and black slacks, with his dark brown hair and suntanned complexion, it was no wonder that he had been all but invisible in the dark. His broad shoulders and tapered waist spoke of a man in peak condition.

Yet it was the intelligence in his deep-set gray eyes that most struck her. He was not a man to be underestimated on any level.

"I don't understand," Mollie said, almost to herself. "You don't seem like a thief... or worse."

He didn't have to ask her what she meant; attacks on women were all too common in any large city. A sudden flash of insight into what she must have thought when he grabbed her made him feel unaccustomedly regretful. He was sorry enough to have frightened her, but even more so to have made her aware of her special vulnerability as a young and very attractive woman.

It wasn't like him to feel regret. Annoyed, he swiftly replaced the shelves and the supplies they had held.

Nothing was left to indicate that there was anything unusual behind the wall.

Gruffly, he said, "Who I am doesn't matter, at least not until we establish who you are. Let's go." He took hold of her arm again and left the supply closet. So quickly did he walk that Mollie almost had to run to keep up with him.

"I'm not a dog on a leash, you know. And I've got enough sense to know that I can't get away from you, so you'll be perfectly safe letting go of me."

The idea that she might pose some danger to him was beginning to amuse him, whereas a short time before he had taken it very seriously. Now that he'd had a chance to see her in a clearer light—both figuratively and literally—he was almost convinced that she wasn't what he had suspected. But that didn't mean she wouldn't have to be dealt with, one way or another.

"All right," he said equably. "But if you have any ideas about trying to get help, put them out of your mind. You wouldn't like what would happen."

Mollie believed him. While she couldn't claim to be any great expert where men were concerned, she knew enough to understand that he meant exactly what he said. For some unknown reason, he was determined to find out who she was. What he would do after that, she didn't care to think.

"My office is on the eighth floor," she said as they waited for the service elevator that would take them to the lobby floor. Despite his warning, she couldn't help remembering that at this hour there would be a guard on duty to sign late arrivals or departures in and out of the building. She would only have to cry out and...

And what? She had experienced for herself the near-lethal force with which the man could act when he chose. For all she knew, he might be carrying any number of weapons and be perfectly willing to use them. Her vivid imagination immediately sprang into overdrive.

She had a quick mental picture of a TV reporter, microphone in hand, talking into a battery of cameras as he described the massacre that had occurred in the lobby of the country's oldest and most respected bank.

It would be a sensation complete with screaming headlines, shrieking sirens and gawking crowds. All because of her. Caught up in her vivid imaginings, she shivered.

"Something wrong?" Eagle asked as the elevator door opened on the lobby. He had been watching the play of emotions across her expressive features and had a fair idea of what she'd been thinking. His question was purely rhetorical, intended to distract her from such grim thoughts.

"Wh-what?" she asked dazedly, only to recover herself quickly and glare at him. "Wrong? Of course not. What could possibly be wrong? There I was, minding my own business, trying to get some work done—which, incidentally, was for one of the bank's partners—and some madman dressed all in black like

an Old West gunslinger comes out of nowhere and
tries to choke me.''

"I wasn't trying to do that," he responded mildly.
"If I had been, you wouldn't have known anything
more about it."

Mollie swallowed hastily and kept her eyes glued
straight ahead. They had to wait several minutes for
the elevator that would take them to her floor.

She could see the guard only a short distance away,
his back turned to them. The temptation to call out to
him was almost irresistible but dread of the consequences kept her silent.

"Smart girl," Eagle murmured approvingly as they
got into the elevator and the doors slid shut. He
pushed the button for the eighth floor at the same time
that he released her. Mollie instantly moved as far
away from him as she could.

"Woman," she muttered. "It's rude and patroniz-
ing to call women girls."

"I beg your pardon," he said gravely, inclining his
head, but not completely hiding his smile. "These days
one can never be sure when the transition occurs. You
don't look all that far removed from girlhood."

"Well, I am," she assured him, "and you'd be
smart to remember that. I'm nobody to push
around."

Eagle laughed, the same rich sound she had heard
before. She flushed and shot him a look that would
have shriveled a lesser man.

"Go on, be like that, but don't say I didn't warn you. You'll be sorry you tangled with me."

"I'm quaking in my boots," Eagle assured her, still grinning. "Which is tough, since I'm not wearing any."

"Men like you," Mollie told him loftily, "always wear boots, if only in their own minds."

"That sounds very profound," he said as the door slid open on the eighth floor. "But I'm not sure what it means."

Neither was she, though she wasn't about to admit that. Instead she walked stiffly ahead of him toward the double glass doors that led to the library. At this late hour, when the rest of the staff had gone home, they were locked, but she had the key in her skirt pocket.

A single light burned in her office toward the back the spacious room. To reach it, they walked past the high tiers of books and magazines, the reading tables and the microfilm machines.

"Nice place," Eagle said as he glanced at the well-ordered shelves. He had noted the key earlier, when he searched her, but he'd had no way of knowing what it opened; now it further convinced him that she was who she said.

He was even more certain when she marched confidently into a pleasant office on the door of which was a name plate reading "M. Fletcher, Chief Librarian."

"My purse is in the desk drawer," she said. "If I get it out, will you think I'm going for a gun or something equally melodramatic?"

More from habit than inclination, he stepped in front of her. "Why don't you let me get it?" Having done so, he opened the purse and pulled out a wallet, flipping through it while she stood tight-lipped, watching him.

"Hmm," he said, "driver's license, blood donor's card, library card, and several charge cards all made out to one Mollie Fletcher. Either you're who you say you are or your cover's the best I've seen."

"Will you stop this?" she demanded, at the end of her patience. "I've gone as far as I can to prove who I am, only to keep you from doing God-only-knows-what to me. Now I want a few answers, starting with who you are and what you were doing in that tunnel."

Eagle looked at her steadily for a long moment. Her face was flushed, and her green eyes had darkened to the hue of the sea when a storm lies directly over the horizon. He didn't have to be told that she had been pushed as far as she could go.

The way he saw it, he didn't have very many choices. Having been trained to assess people quickly and accurately, he was certain she wasn't about to let the subject drop, regardless of what she had suggested earlier.

If he tried to simply walk away, she would undoubtedly pursue the matter, if only by returning to the tunnel to explore further. That could lead her into disaster, for which he did not want to be in any way responsible.

On the other hand, if he told her the truth she would immediately be involved, and that, too, might prove deadly.

The silence drew out between them. Mollie was becoming increasingly impatient, but she knew better than to try to rush him. Like Eagle, she was a keen judge of character, though not for the same reasons. With her it was simply an interesting part of life to understand what made other people tick; with him it was a matter of survival.

He accepted that for himself, but now someone else's life might well be on the line, and that was something he hadn't bargained on. Perhaps the best approach might be a compromise between the truth and a lie, something he could say to satisfy her curiosity and keep her from getting any more involved.

Propping himself on the edge of her desk, he unzipped his windbreaker and reached inside. As Mollie stiffened, he said soothingly, "Relax, I'm simply returning the favor."

He drew out his wallet—black calfskin—and handed it to her, opened. She took it while still peering at him suspiciously.

The card he had turned up was his faculty ID. As she read it, her eyes widened. "Sebastian Barnett, History Department, Columbia University. You're a college professor?"

"Guilty. My specialty is early American history."

"Which is how you came to be exploring the tunnel?" Before he could answer, she added, "But why did you attack me the way you did?"

"You scared me," Eagle said with a perfectly straight face.

Mollie snorted in disbelief. "Tell me another one. You weren't scared at all. *I* was the one who was terrified. Not only that, but you knew exactly what to do to knock me out without inflicting any real damage."

"I'm relieved to know you suffered no ill effects."

"Your concern is very touching," Mollie said dryly, "but it doesn't answer my question. What were you doing down there?"

"Looking for something that may or may not be hidden in the tunnel." He smiled apologetically. "I'm afraid it's no more interesting than that." Straightening, he added, "And I'm sorry I frightened you. I hope you'll forgive me?"

The intensity in his silver-gray eyes held hers as she nodded absently. "Of course, but . . ."

Regret lent a soft undertone to his voice. "That's all there is, Mollie Fletcher. I'll be going now."

At the door he paused and looked at her. She was so lovely standing there, with her rosy lips slightly parted and her big eyes full of puzzlement, that it was all he could do not to walk back to her and let his instincts take their natural course.

It had been a long time since he'd met a woman who made him feel like that. He hated to turn away from her, but to do otherwise would be the height of unfairness. She deserved better.

The softness was gone when he said, "Don't go back into the tunnel. It really is dangerous." For good measure, he added, "Besides the rats and snakes, the roof is about to give way. You could be trapped, and no one would find you until it was too late."

Mollie paled at the thought, as he had intended. "Are you going back?"

"Forget about it," he said, refusing to answer more directly. "And me." With that, he turned and walked out the door. She heard his footsteps recede down the hallway, until there was only silence.

Fat chance that she would forget, Mollie thought somberly. That was like telling her to forget a... Come to think of it, she couldn't find anything to compare him to. Nothing in her experience had prepared her to deal with him. Which was just as well, since he clearly did not intend to have anything further to do with her.

His loss, she grumbled to herself as she decided that the partner's inquiry could wait until Monday after all. She was going home to feed her cat, take a hot bath and find something more interesting to think about than the mysterious man who had passed so abruptly through her life, leaving in his wake all sorts of unresolved feelings she didn't quite know how to cope with.

Chapter 3

The trouble with you, Mollie," Lisa Hardesty was saying, "is that you aren't aggressive enough when it comes to men. You've got this image in your head of the perfect prince charming, and you don't want to settle for anything less."

"Not true," Mollie insisted after she had swallowed a bite of her tuna fish sandwich.

It was the following Monday. The two friends were having lunch in an empty office before going shopping. Lisa wanted to visit a new boutique that had recently opened near the bank, and Mollie had agreed to go along, even though she generally found shopping boring.

"I'd no more want a perfect man," she went on, "than I'd aspire to be perfect myself. All I want is someone intelligent, reliable and kind, with a good sense of humor. Is that too much to ask for?"

"It shouldn't be," Lisa agreed. "But in today's world, guys like that are scarcer than hens' teeth. You may have to lower your standards, at least long enough to get in a little practice."

"No thanks. I'm not interested in putting any notches on my bed posts. I'd rather be alone than be involved with a man I didn't care about."

"I wish I felt like that," Lisa said. "But every time I break up with a guy, I feel panicky and at loose ends until I meet someone new."

Mollie nodded sympathetically; she and Lisa had talked about this before, and she understood her friend's point of view even though she thought it unfortunate. Not everyone was as content with solitary pursuits as she was, and even for her, a life without someone important to share it with was less than complete.

Lisa finished her salad—she was more scrupulous about watching her weight than Mollie was—and tossed the debris into a nearby waste can. "Let's go buy something absolutely wild. That always cheers me up."

"You buy, I'll look," Mollie said as they left the office and walked toward the elevators. "Wild clothes don't exactly suit my personality."

"You might be surprised," Lisa told her as they left the bank and turned left on Pearl Street. The lunchtime crowd was heavy, as usual, thronging the nar-

row, twisting streets. Horns blared as harassed traffic
police tried to keep clogged streams of traffic moving.

The women slipped past a delivery truck blocking
an intersection, wove around a taxi, and avoided a hot
dog truck. Thunderstorms over the weekend had done
little to relieve the sticky heat still settled over the city.

Most of the men they passed were in shirt-sleeves,
the women in thin cotton dresses. Condensation from
countless air conditioners created little puddles every
few yards. They stepped over one to enter the boutique.

"Lovely," Lisa murmured as cool, dry air struck
them. Immediately invigorated, she began to browse
through a rack of dresses marked "On Sale."

"Some sale," Mollie murmured as she checked a
price tag. "Who can afford this stuff?"

"Who can't?" Lisa countered. She held up an amber silk dress that dramatically offset her pale blond
features. "With the competition for men in this town,
you have to look fabulous all the time, otherwise you
never get any attention. Not," she added with a wry
smile, "that you have to worry. Any time you decide
to, you can shuck that camouflage and get any man
you want."

Mollie laughed. "I don't think so. Besides, my
clothes aren't camouflage; they're what I like."

"At the moment, but mark my words, when the day
comes that you meet a man who interests you, you'll

be shopping for a new wardrobe so quick you won't know what hit you.''

"Really." Mollie glanced absently along the rack, then reached out tentatively and touched an emerald green sweater that had caught her eye. "And what do you think I should buy, if that great day ever arrives?''

"Something like that sweater," Lisa said promptly, "and..." She paused for a moment, scanning the rack. "And these great slacks, perfect for your coloring.''

She handed the russet suede slacks to Mollie, and for good measure added the sweater. "Here, go try these on, just to see how they look.''

"There's no point," Mollie protested.

"'Course there is. It will satisfy my curiosity, and maybe start you thinking in a different direction.'' Before Mollie could argue further, Lisa took the clothes from her and handed them to a sales clerk. "My friend wants to try these on.''

"Certainly, if you'll follow me...''

Feeling it would be foolish to refuse, Mollie did as the woman said and was shown to a dressing room. Lisa lingered to continue looking around. "I'll be right behind you," she called after Mollie, "so don't try chickening out.''

Resigned, Mollie thanked the sales clerk and shut the door of the dressing room. Glancing at the clothes now neatly hung on a hook near the full-length mirror, she had to admit that they were attractive. Most of her wardrobe was pretty ordinary. It wouldn't hurt to brighten it up a bit.

Having removed her skirt and blouse, she pulled the sweater over her head, in the process undoing the pins that held her hair in place. With a small exclamation of impatience, she yanked her hair free of the collar and let it fall over her shoulders.

The sweater was woven of a combination of silk and cotton. It was so thin that she felt she was barely wearing anything at all. The slacks were next, slipping over her tapered legs with a deliciously cool sensation that made her shiver slightly.

She stared thoughtfully at herself in the mirror. Maybe Lisa had a point. In brighter clothes that weren't as loose as those she usually wore, she really did look different. The sweater clung to her full breasts and slim waist, while the snugly fitted slacks emphasized her slender hips and long legs. She tossed her hair back with a faint smile, wondering what great-great-Aunt Amelia would say.

"Wow! I thought I knew what I meant when I said clothes would make a difference, but I really had no idea."

Mollie turned and smiled at Lisa, who had poked her head into the dressing room. "Satisfied?"

"You're not surprised."

The shoulders beneath the emerald wool rose and fell. "I've known how I looked for years, since I was thirteen, to be precise. I just don't see any reason to play it up."

Lisa leaned against the wall and openly stared at her friend. "You must realize that there are women who would kill to look like you."

"Which is their problem, not mine. Now, let me get out of this stuff."

"You're not going to buy it?" Lisa was genuinely surprised.

"Why should I? It's hardly the sort of outfit I'd wear to the office, and I've got plenty of casual clothes already." But even as she spoke, Mollie was reconsidering.

A glance in the mirror confirmed that the sweater and slacks might have been made for her. They brought out the deep vividness of her eyes and played up the auburn highlights in her luxurious hair.

And they made her think about something that she had tried unsuccessfully all weekend to get out of her mind: she wanted to see Sebastian Barnett again.

He interested her in a way no other man had ever done, partly, she supposed, because of the exotic circumstances in which they had met. She was no more immune to the appeal of danger and mystery than any other woman would be, but she also knew herself well enough to be certain that her interest in Sebastian went far deeper.

After all, they shared a love of history as well as an inclination to venture where others would hesitate to go. Once she had gotten over her initial fear of him,

she had sensed a quiet strength that was the masculine version of her own.

A slight smile lifted the corners of her mouth as she
admitted to herself that intellectual compatibility was
not the sum total of his appeal. What she lacked in
experience she made up for in instincts, and those were
telling her that she would be a fool to let Sebastian
walk out of her life.

Which brought her to the problem of how to get in
touch with him again. After she and Lisa had returned to the bank, she put the shopping bag with her
new clothes away and settled down to give some serious thought to her problem.

Fortunately it was very quiet in the library, and she
had no pressing business to attend to; the partner who
had been responsible for her being in the sub-basement
the previous Friday had decided he didn't need the information after all, and all the other inquiries on her
desk were routine.

Chin cupped in her hand, she stared out through the
window overlooking Wall Street and wondered how
she could set about seducing Sebastian Barnett. The
very topic of her thoughts gave her a secret pleasure,
not unlike the experience of lying under her favorite
afghan on a rainy evening while watching a special old
movie and eating the better part of a box of choco-
lates.

Such indulgences were all the more enjoyable for
being so uncharacteristic; in the case of her present

preoccupation, she could not remember ever before setting out with such a goal in mind.

The seduction of Sebastian. It had a nice ring to it, even as a little voice in the back of her mind warned that the seducing might be on the other side. Brief though her acquaintance with him had been, she had seen enough to know that he had not spent all his time in classrooms and study carrels.

On the contrary, there was a hint of cynicism and world-weariness in his manner that challenged her. She realized that it would be worth a great deal to her to shake his composure and see what might fall out.

Her brother had told her once that all her efforts to make life safe and well-ordered were a response to the hidden, impetuous side of her nature, which she did not want to recognize but could never fully deny. Thinking about that now, she had to admit that he might have been right, because pursuing Sebastian was certainly neither safe nor well-ordered. Yet she had made up her mind to do it.

How did one seduce a man, presuming that was her long-term objective and that she wouldn't get cold feet at the last minute? To begin with, there had to be bait, which should theoretically be herself. In this case she suspected that would not be enough.

Not that she had any real doubts about her attractiveness when she made even the most moderate effort. What she did doubt was that she could on her own overcome her quarry's apparent reluctance to have anything further to do with her. Hadn't he, after all, walked out of her life without a backward glance?

A lesser woman might have found that discouraging. Mollie, having once made up her mind to pursue a particular course, was not so easily turned away from it. What she needed was a plausible reason for seeking Sebastian out, after which she would trust nature to take its course.

He was interested, if not in her, in the tunnel on top of which she sat. He had said there might be something in the tunnel that he had hoped to find. That gave her a place to begin; if she could figure out what he'd been looking for, maybe she could come up with some useful suggestions about where it might be.

The answers, if they existed at all, had to be in the sub-basement, where every piece of paper, every fact and figure ever to pass through the hallowed halls of Cabot Brothers, was interred. For more than a hundred and fifty years, the bank had existed, growing steadily bigger and stronger, enduring catastrophes both natural and man-made that had changed the world but affected the bank very little.

Cabot Brothers and the Constitution, that's what the partners liked to say would always exist so long as the nation lived. The Constitution was the cornerstone of liberty; Cabot Brothers, and a handful of other institutions like it, were the fulcrum of power.

There were secrets buried within the bowels of the sedately elegant building. Some of them Mollie had already stumbled across in the course of her duties;

others were still hidden from her, but if any of them had to do with the tunnel and what it might hold, she intended to find them out without delay.

Which meant another visit to the sub-basement. She took the freight elevator down and let herself into the section where the archives were kept. She resisted the impulse to enter the utility closet again, though she did peer into it long enough to confirm that the back wall was still snugly in place. No one glancing at it casually could guess what lay behind it.

Her footsteps rang on the stone floor as she walked down the rows of metal files, which gave way eventually to the wooden cabinets of an earlier era. Each was neatly labeled in fading copperplate: 1908 ... 1892 ... 1876 ... 1854 ... and so on back to the very origins of the bank in 1817.

At the last cabinet, Mollie paused. She had looked in it once before, prompted by idle curiosity, and had discovered bundles of documents so yellowed and frayed with age that they threatened to fall apart at the lightest touch.

There were account books in which the ink had faded to near illegibility, letters festooned with seals that had long ago cracked, receipts for deposits and withdrawals in the hodgepodge of currencies that had sustained the infant republic during its earliest years.

Mollie surveyed the frail remnants of the past hesitantly. She was loathe to risk damaging them with no clear purpose in mind, but she really had no idea where her attention might better be directed. What she needed was information about the building that had once occupied this site.

Since one of the proudest boasts of the bank's directors was that it had been in the same location from the first day of its existence, it stood to reason that these earliest records would tell her who had owned the first building, and perhaps even what purpose it had been used for.

Far sooner than she had hoped, she found the information she was looking for. It appeared in a letter to a cabinetmaker evidently hired to outfit the new bank with furnishings suitable to its status. Dated September 6, 1817, the letter read in part:

From Master Duncan Phyfe, cabinetmaker, to be received for the sum of fifteen pounds sterling, one mahogany and satinwood desk and chair of same. Payment to be made upon delivery to Cabot Brothers Bank, at the address formerly belonging to the Waverly Trading Company.

At least those early Cabots had enjoyed excellent taste, Mollie thought as she carefully turned the notice over and went on to the next document. Duncan Phyfe had emerged as one of the preeminent furniture makers of the nineteenth century; his works were prized by collectors everywhere. If the particular desk and chair in question still existed, they were undoubtedly worth many hundreds of times their original price.

So the bank had taken over a building previously occupied by the Waverly Trading Company, whatever that had been. Though she didn't know any more specifics, she felt she was at least getting closer to the truth about the tunnel.

A sense of burgeoning excitement flowed through her as she considered what it must have been like back in those days, shortly after the end of the War of 1812, scant decades since the Revolution.

It was a time when constant rivalries between England and France had often caused the distinction between trading and smuggling to be ignored. She had no difficulty believing that canny traders might well have seen the advantage of a secret conduit from their headquarters to the docks.

How much of this did Sebastian know? Probably at least some, since there were other sources of such information besides the bank records. She would need more to justify going to him.

And she found it before she had looked much further. The letter that caught her eye was as badly faded as all the rest, but the script was slightly less elaborate and therefore easier to read. She scanned it slowly, not wanting to miss anything. The sender wrote:

I have this day spoken with the honorable Mr. Monroe, who assures me there is no impediment to the sale of the property, and that the arrangements may proceed forthwith, as business in the capital keeps him fully occupied, and he is anxious to disengage himself of his holdings here.

Monroe? There was only one Monroe in history that
Mollie had ever heard of, the fifth president of the
United States. What an astonishing coincidence it
would be if he had been a principle in the Waverly
Trading Company, although now that she thought of
it, the possibility wasn't really so unlikely.

She knew that James Monroe had been a lawyer in
New York before moving on to politics. As for the lack
of any reference to him as president in the letter, that
too wasn't so surprising, since it hadn't been until the
twentieth century that presidents were treated with
particular regard.

Here was a tidbit she could legitimately take to Sebastian, since as an historian he was bound to find
even a possible connection to a former president interesting. Smiling to herself, she carefully slid the letter into a manila file she had brought along in case she
found anything useful.

Sebastian would have to understand, of course, that
the letter was the property of the bank and must be
returned. If he wanted to pursue the matter, he could
contact her employers. Given his credentials, she suspected that they wouldn't deny him access to the archives, where she would be happy to assist him in what
would undoubtedly be a very time-consuming search.

All in all, it wasn't a bad plan. She was tempted to
call Lisa and boast to her of it, if only to show that she
wasn't completely inept when it came to men, but she

held off, preferring to keep such a private matter to herself.

Instead, she called Columbia University and asked to speak to someone in the history department, who could tell her when Sebastian would be in. It seemed that he had classes three days a week and was available for conferences on Tuesday afternoons.

Mollie had quite a bit of vacation time coming to her, so she decided to take the next day off. She slept late, tidied up her apartment, took a long bath, and finally, around noon, dressed in her new clothes. Looking at herself in the full-length mirror on her closet door, she smiled.

Her sense of humor was piqued by the thought of what he would say when he saw her, and what he would do. For one of the few times in her life, she appreciated the beauty that gave her a certain power over men.

As she locked the apartment door and ran quickly down the stairs, she wondered if she hadn't inherited more from great-great-Aunt Amelia than she had hitherto wanted to admit.

Chapter 4

"And so," Sebastian was saying, "we see, in the early industrialization of the United States, the foundation being laid for what was to be a major economic shift in the years immediately following the Civil War."

A bell rang in the distance, signaling the end of class. It was a mark of the respect with which his students regarded him that no one moved.

"Kindly read Chapter Three before our next meeting, and remember that I want to see each of you to discuss the topics of your papers."

A good-natured groan met this last instruction as the students—about two dozen of them—rose and gathered their things together. Most of them trooped out of the classroom, but a few lingered to question Sebastian about the just-concluded lecture.

He responded to their inquiries politely but briefly before excusing himself, much to the disappointment of the several young ladies who vied for his attention. This early in the summer session, he already had a fair idea of who was taking the course for its own sake and who wasn't.

He was enough used to the latter to be neither displeased nor flattered by what he knew some other members of the history faculty referred to behind his back as "Sebastian's groupies." Besides, he wasn't above enjoying a pretty face gazing at him raptly while he lectured, even if he sometimes wondered how many were actually listening.

At the moment, however, he had far more immediate concerns. As he crossed the quadrangle toward his office, he thought back to the phone call he'd received early that morning on the secure line in his apartment. Messenger, his control within the organization, had been quite direct.

"We've had another letter," he had told Eagle. "The demands are spelled out even more closely, as are the consequences should we fail to fulfill them. Some action will have to be taken very soon."

"Have we any more reason to believe they actually have the document?" Eagle had asked.

"No, but Alpha has decided that the risk is too great to simply presume they're bluffing."

'Alpha' was the President of the United States. If he was already involved, the organization must seriously doubt its ability to contain the matter. This was quickly shaping up into a full-blown crisis.

"Please tell Alpha that a further effort to confirm the document's whereabouts will be made tonight," Eagle had told his control.

There had been a moment's hesitation on the other end of the line; then, very quietly, Messenger had said, "I see. Be careful."

He hardly needed to be told that, Sebastian thought, even though he had appreciated the sentiment. It was rare that anyone within the organization expressed concern for a colleague, perhaps because some level of danger was always present in everything they did. To think about it constantly was to invite the slow, insidious corruption of fear, leading ultimately to an end to usefulness.

Sebastian was determined to avoid that. He had been a member of the organization for ten years, since he was twenty-four, and in that time had learned to live with the secret past of his life without allowing it to overwhelm him.

Yet there were times when he wondered what he would be like if he had chosen a different course. The men and women he worked with at the university were aware of some subtle difference about him that set him apart.

Unlike most of them, he did not have a family. There were no pictures of a wife or children in his office, nor did he turn up at university events with a girlfriend in tow.

While his associates spent their vacations in Europe or on the Cape, he either taught the summer session, a chore he could easily have escaped given his tenured status, or disappeared on an assignment for the organization. This summer he was doing both.

In his office, he shut the door and put his feet up on the desk. As casually dressed as his students in khakis and a work shirt, he nevertheless exuded an aura of self-containment and confidence no younger man could match. His body, honed in rigorous exercise that was as much a tool of survival as any weapon he might carry, was lean in the legs and hips, broad at the torso and shoulders.

Naked, the lithe strength of his muscles and the taut grace of his movements were the only obvious clues to his other life. The women he had been with, none of whom he had ever taken into his confidence, had invariably sensed something unusual about him without being able to define it. His physique was easily as well developed as those of men who worked out at health clubs or regularly practiced athletics, yet it was also different.

Perhaps it was just as well that none of them had ever understood what made it so, namely that his strength was not the result of personal vanity or anything so innocent as pleasure in a sport. He was strong simply because in his world the weak perished. There was no room for failure, no margin for error. A moment's slip was enough to result in death.

Which was why he could not afford any distractions, no matter how appealing they might be. He sighed as he leaned back in his chair with his arms folded behind his head. There were plans to be made, a strategy to be decided on, but he found that he could think of little except Mollie Fletcher.

She had intruded on his thoughts constantly over the last few days. Even as he told himself that he had been right to walk away from her, he couldn't help but regret it. The beauty and strength he had sensed in her drew him almost irresistibly. Worse yet, they made him aware of how long he had been alone.

That was by his choice, and until now he had had no reason to regret it. Yet suddenly he found himself wondering what it would be like to be free to pick up the phone and call her, let her into his life without worrying about the consequences to them both.

He could do it, of course, when his present assignment was over, but how long would they have before his duties in the organization intruded? He had long ago decided it was unfair to become involved with any woman on other than the most casual basis, which he knew instinctively Mollie would not accept.

There was something about her.... He smiled as he thought of it. She was old-fashioned in a way he couldn't fully grasp but still enjoyed. She made him think of other, simpler days, before his spirit had lost the innocence hers still retained.

Which was the last thing he should have been thinking of just then. His initial foray into the tunnel had been inconclusive, because he had broken it off when he realized he was being followed. It was imperative that the tunnel be thoroughly explored and an assessment made of the situation.

He was getting up to leave, intending to return to his apartment and prepare for what he would do that night, when a knock on the door stopped him. He frowned, hoping whoever it was wouldn't be long-winded.

"Come in."

Mollie opened the door hesitantly. He didn't sound very welcoming, more like distracted verging on impatient. Still, she had come this far and wasn't about to turn away now. Stepping into the office, she smiled.

"Hi, I hope I'm not interrupting. . . ."

Sebastian stared at her in silence for a moment, his features giving away none of his thoughts, which was just as well, since they would undoubtedly have startled, if not embarrassed, her.

Having been so recently regretting that he couldn't see her again, her sudden appearance made him wonder for a moment if his imagination might be playing tricks on him. Not only did she seem to be right there in front of him, but she looked even lovelier than he remembered.

His forehead knitted together as he considered that. She had done something to herself...let down her hair for a start, so that it flowed over her shoulders, catching the light in silken strands. And her clothes were different. They fit better and played up her coloring.

All his warning signals were at full tilt. When he had first seen her, she had been attractive enough to at least dent his concentration. Now she was far more than that, and he was instantly wary. Whatever she wanted, he meant to get her out of there fast.

"How are you, Miss Fletcher?" he asked courteously, holding out a chair for her. She might have been in the habit of dropping by his office every day, so little reaction did he show.

Mollie was inwardly disappointed, but she told herself not to be discouraged. Certainly she hadn't expected him to put out the welcome mat for her.

"I won't keep you, Professor Barnett," she said as she sat down. "I'm here because I came across a piece of information that I thought might be of help to you. That is, if you're still interested in the tunnel?"

At his subdued nod, she handed over the file containing the letter she had found. "It seems to indicate that someone named Monroe, possibly *the* James Monroe, was a part owner of the property where the bank now stands. It was occupied by a trading company, which could account for the existence of the tunnel."

"The Waverly Company," Eagle said as he studied the letter. Long experience with such artifacts made it possible for him to read it quickly, while giving away none of the inner excitement he felt. Did she have any idea of the magnitude of her discovery? If she was right, his mission was suddenly even more urgent than before.

Mollie was mildly deflated that not all of her news was a surprise, but he was occupied enough with the letter to reassure her that her visit was not completely wasted. When he put it down at last, she said, "Do you think it's really possible that President Monroe was involved in all this?"

He smiled at her eagerness. Even with all that he'd seen and done over the years, he had never lost the initial sense of excitement that had brought him to the study of the past. Apparently, she shared it.

"Anything's possible," he said as noncommitally as he could manage. "At any rate, it was very thoughtful of you to bring this. I'll have a copy made, if you don't mind, so that I can return this to you immediately."

"Won't you need to authenticate the original?"

"If it ever became necessary to prove Monroe's involvement, but that hardly seems likely." Deliberately he said, "The tunnel is simply a curiosity, nothing more."

"You said you were looking for something in it."

"Old tools, that's all. I have an interest in the manufacturing techniques of the early nineteenth century." He made that sound as pedantic and boring as he could manage in the hope that she would lose interest.

Instead, she nodded brightly and said, "I think it's fascinating that the site where the bank now sits may have been a haven for smugglers at one time."

Eagle raised an eyebrow in a gesture he knew had withered many an overeager student or faculty member. "Smugglers? Where did you get that idea?"

Mollie shrugged, refusing to be deflected by his skepticism. "It stands to reason, doesn't it? After all, throughout the Revolution and the War of 1812, smuggling was an absolute necessity. The country couldn't have survived without it."

"By the way," she added, "did you know the bank was founded in 1817, shortly after the war some call the Second Revolution? Maybe whatever you're looking for dates from then."

That was coming perilously close to the truth, so much so that Sebastian had no choice but to move to stop her. He stood up and looked pointedly at his wrist watch. "This is all very interesting, Miss Fletcher, and I do appreciate your stopping by. But if you'll excuse me, I have a class."

Mollie knew he was lying; the history department secretary had told her he was free all afternoon. That he would deliberately mislead her hurt more than she would have expected. It made her wonder if she had been wrong about him.

Summoning her dignity, she stood up, and even managed to smile. "Forgive me; I had no intention of keeping you. If you'd have the letter copied..."

"Of course." They walked together out into the reception area, where the secretaries sat. He handed the letter to a plump older woman with a kindly face. "Would you mind duplicating this for me, Sheila?"

Generally such delicate documents weren't subjected to photocopying, because the light used could damage them, but he didn't think just once would hurt.

She assured him that she'd be happy to take care of it and hurried off, leaving Sebastian and Mollie alone again, except for the two other secretaries, who cast curious glances their way. "Let's wait outside," he said, taking her arm and guiding her toward the hallway.

The gesture reminded her of his behavior the previous Friday, and she stiffened. He ignored that until they were away from watching eyes; then he dropped his hand abruptly.

"I'm sorry," he said. "You must think I do nothing but haul people around."

"The possibility had occurred to me." His apology made her feel slightly less self-conscious. Despite his apparent eagerness to be rid of her, he had been watching her with an intensity that made her acutely aware of herself. She had the feeling that he had missed nothing of her changed appearance, and that his response to it was everything she could have wished—except that he chose to deny it.

She had no idea why that might be the case, except that he clearly wanted nothing further to do with her. Living in New York as she did, she came in contact frequently with men who had no use for women except occasionally as friends. She had no difficulty either identifying or accepting such a preference, but she was also certain it wasn't what motivated Sebastian. He was, for want of a better phrase, all man, and she was woman enough to apppreciate that.

But he was also very stubborn, almost as stubborn as she herself.

The secretary met them in the hallway and returned the original of the letter, handing the copy to Sebastian. She gave Mollie a motherly smile before returning to her desk, leaving them once again alone.

It was very quiet in the hallway. Outside, she could hear the distant sounds of traffic and the voices of students calling to each other. But here, inside the old stone building that had seen generations of scholars come and go, time seemed to have slowed to a crawl.

She was standing very close to Sebastian, near enough be aware of the nearly electrical resonance in the air between them. She had read about such things in books, but had never taken them seriously before. Now she had no choice but to do so.

Beautiful as Mollie was, soft and yielding as she could appear, she possessed a backbone of steel. For the first time in her life, she truly wanted a man. That he did not seem to want her, or at least didn't want to admit it, would not deter her.

None of which meant that she was fool enough to throw herself at him. Even in these supposedly enlightened days, it was the wise woman who let the man be the aggressor, or at least let him think he was.

An old saying flitted through her mind—"a man chases a woman until he is caught." She would let Sebastian Barnett create his own trap, and then she would be only too happy to catch him in it.

"I'd better be going now," she said demurely. "If you do turn up anything in the tunnel, perhaps you'd let me know about it."

He nodded, knowing that if he found what he was looking for, no one outside of a very select few would ever be told. "I'll walk you out," he said, surprising himself. There was no good reason to prolong his time with her; it would only make the parting more difficult.

Yet once they were on the sidewalk in front of the main building, he couldn't regret having wanted a few more minutes with her. In the dim light of the hallway she had been beautiful, but in the bright sunshine she was even lovelier. He could easily become fascinated by the radiance of her hair, the soft flush of her cheeks, the deep, mysterious green of her eyes.

"Is something wrong?" Mollie asked softly. His preoccupation had not eluded her. She was flattered by it, but also disquieted. If he really found her so interesting, why was he sending her on her way?

No matter that he was, she decided. The course of her life had never been determined by other people, only by herself. Taking the initiative had long ago become second nature.

"Good luck with the tunnel," she said. He was nodding absently when she added, "And if I have any luck, of course I'll let you know."

"What," he asked after a long moment, "are you talking about?"

"The tunnel, naturally. I'm going to explore it myself."

"I told you it was too dangerous."

"Yes, I know you did, and I've thought about that. I've decided that with the proper precautions, I'll be fine."

"You're wrong," Eagle said. A shutter had dropped down over his face. His eyes revealed nothing, and his voice was completely without expression. Behind that impenetrable mask, his mind was working feverishly.

Somehow she had to be stopped from venturing into the tunnel alone. The thought of what might happen to her if she did made his blood run cold.

Quickly he considered his options. He could have her fired, so she would no longer have access to the building. Or he could have her detained, held at one of the organization's safe houses until the danger was past.

Both were fairly extreme solutions that might well raise more questions than they answered. And there was nothing to say that she wouldn't attempt to pursue the matter afterward, perhaps even going far enough to make the organization decide she was a threat to security.

He didn't want to think about where that could lead. Though he completely agreed with the purpose of the organization, believing as he did that freedom had to be preserved by more than just words, he knew that sometimes the methods called for were as harsh as anything used by the other side. The thought of Mollie falling into the hands of the organization's "clean up" squad made his stomach twist. He would do anything to protect her from them.

Which meant that he also had to protect her from herself.

There was always the possibility that she was bluffing, but a careful look into her gold-flecked emerald eyes convinced him that she wasn't. She met his gaze unflinchingly, letting him take in the full measure of the challenge she represented.

"All right," he said at length. "I'm not going to pretend for a moment that I like it, but you can explore the tunnel with me."

Chapter 5

That's very nice of you," Mollie said, "but I'm not sure that I wouldn't rather go alone." She was speaking purely out of bravado, having no intention of entering the tunnel alone again.

Sebastian suspected she was bluffing, but chose not to call her on it. There was a chance she would feel compelled to carry through, and that he could not allow.

"You'll go down with me or not at all," he said flatly.

Mollie's green eyes widened ingenuously. She was enjoying standing up to him; it made her feel very daring, but also perfectly safe, since she had no doubt that he meant exactly what he said. A mixture of curiosity and mischievousness prompted her to ask, "How do you propose to stop me?"

"However I have to."

Mollie swallowed the lump that had suddenly developed in her throat. Her enjoyment of the situation was fast fading as she came smack up against his implacability. Still she refused to back down. "That sounds a little melodramatic."

He shrugged. "Take it anyway you want to; just don't make the mistake of thinking we're both bluffing."

"Both? I have no idea what you mean."

Sebastian had been having a hard time keeping a straight face, and now he gave up the effort altogether. With her magnificent eyes gleaming and her petal-soft skin flushed, she looked at once delightfully feminine and fiercely determined.

That combination of sensuality and strength could not fail to appeal to him. He found himself hard-pressed not to reach out to her.

Years of deeply imbued training and discipline stopped him. He had a job to do, and she was threatening to complicate it by going off on her own. On the other hand, it was just possible that she might actually be a help.

The thought of using her had occurred to him earlier. He had almost dismissed it outright because of the danger he would be putting her in, but it was not his way to overlook any possible options, and because of that he had gone so far as to request a report on her from the organization.

It had come through the previous day, produced with the usual efficiency that never failed to both impress and dismay him. He wondered if the great mass of ordinary people had any idea how much information was available on them simply by connecting with the correct computers.

He knew, for instance, how long Mollie had been with Cabot Brothers, how much she made, how much was in her savings account and how much she owed on her charge cards.

He knew she was a rather substantial buyer of books and occasionally rented videocassettes. She had gone to the Caribbean the year before, gave regularly to charity, had had her appendix removed at the age of eight, and had never been treated for a social disease.

In short, he knew far more than he felt he had any right to know. Ordinarily, he would have pushed aside his qualms at such an invasion of privacy, justifying it as necessary under the circumstances. But this time he had trouble doing that, perhaps because he would have preferred to get to know her in a very different way.

If life had taught him anything, it was not to regret what could not be changed. He had a difficult, dangerous job to do, and, like it or not, she couldn't be allowed to jeopardize its success.

"Believe me, Mollie," he said softly, "there is absolutely no possibility of your going into that tunnel alone. I think we both know that, so let's quit kidding around and get down to business. I'm going in tonight. If you want to come along, you'll have to be ready on time."

"And when is that?"

He hesitated a moment, not taking his eyes from her face. "One A.M."

Her response pleased him; she masked her surprise almost instantly. But that did not prevent her from asking the most obvious question. "Why on earth would you want to go then?"

"I like to work at night," he said, straight-faced.

Mollie opened her mouth to make some suitable reply, then thought better of it. If he wanted to believe she was that gullible, fine with her. She'd enjoy all the more discovering what he was really up to.

"One A.M." she said serenely. "Where shall we meet?"

"I'll pick you up at your apartment." He remembered to ask her for the address, even though he already knew it. As she turned to leave, he called after her. "Wear something sensible."

She smiled at him over her shoulder. "Not what I've got on now?"

The grooves in his cheeks deepened with male appreciation. Reluctantly, he shook his head. "Jeans and a sweatshirt would be better."

"I'll see what I can come up with," she assured him, wondering how long it would take her to go through

her wardrobe and find something both attractive and
practical.

Sebastian had no such problem; clothes were the
furthest thing from his mind as he unchained his bi-
cycle from the rack in front of the history building.
His apartment was some two miles away on the other
side of town. He considered the trip back and forth to
be mildly good exercise, but no substitute for a real
workout.

Adroitly threading the Italian racer through
bumper-to-bumper traffic, he ran over the preparations he needed to complete for the coming night. Almost everything was already taken care of, but it was
his habit to check and double-check every aspect of a
mission. More than once that had saved his life.

Back in the spacious condominium he owned on an
upper floor of a building overlooking Central Park, he
dropped the pack containing his books and lecture
notes in the den and went into the bedroom to change.

Attired in white cotton trousers and a loose matching jacket tied with a black sash, he went through a
series of increasingly rigorous exercises designed to
bring all his senses to peak alertness.

Forty-five minutes later, when his body was coated
with a fine sheen of sweat, he headed for the shower.
He stood under it until all traces of his exertions were
gone, then dried off and returned to the bedroom.

There he lay down and, after priming his internal
alarm clock to wake him in five hours, fell immediately into a deep sleep. Precisely five hours later he

awoke suitably refreshed and began to lay out his equipment.

In addition to the black cord pants and thin black turtleneck, he added a coil of fishing line, a pair of leather gloves, and a slim leather harness that held a perfectly honed stiletto. This last he strapped around his right calf before dressing. A small but very powerful flashlight went into the pocket of his trousers. From the closet he took an elegantly tailored black jacket. Before donning it, he fastened on a shoulder holster and checked the ammunition clip of the Beretta it held.

Slipping his feet into crepe-soled shoes, he glanced around the room. It was large, particularly by Manhattan standards, with floor-to-ceiling windows overlooking the park. A simple pine bed covered by a handmade quilt, which he had replaced after his nap, stood in the center. Nearby were an oak armoire and dresser with the pure lines created by the Shaker craftsmen. A braided rug covered the floor, and several paintings of the primitive school were on the walls.

Nothing was out of place; nothing showed that he was anything other than the professor of history he claimed to be. Were he to leave this room and never return, no one would be able to discern from it that he had also lived an entirely different life in the shadows.

Unless they found the false panel in the closet and, behind it, the collection of weapons from which he had chosen the items he would carry that night.

Thinking of what those weapons might be used for brought him to the subject of Mollie. Uncharacteristically, he was having second thoughts about allowing her to come along.

His reasons for doing so remained valid, and he was relatively confident of his ability to protect her should the need arise, but it was the slight yet unavoidable possibility that he might have underestimated the opposition that caused him concern.

It was one thing to place himself in danger, quite another to do it to someone he was rapidly coming to care for.

The solution was obvious, and he hesitated only a split second before opting for it. A glance at his watch showed him that Mollie would not be expecting him for more than an hour yet. Plenty of time to get into the tunnel, find whatever was down there, and get out. She would undoubtedly be upset when she discovered how he had tricked her, but he would deal with that when he had to.

The black Jaguar he had purchased recently was parked in the underground garage. Strangers to Manhattan liked to think that the city never slept, but in fact midtown and the financial district were almost empty at this hour.

He reached the area near Cabot Brothers quickly and parked within easy reach of the building, a prudent measure should a swift departure be called for.

Smiling slightly, he wondered how Mollie had imagined he planned to gain access to the building. Perhaps she had thought he would ask her to use her employee identification card to get them in. And he might have done so had she been along, simply to keep her from seeing the slight nod of recognition the security guard gave him when he heard his name. The man had certainly not been told who he was or why he was there, but he had been instructed to cooperate with him fully.

The freight elevator was shut down this late at night, and Sebastian did not ask for it to be turned on for his convenience. He wanted to call as little attention to himself as possible. Taking the stairs, he reached the sub-basement without difficulty and entered the archives room.

A few overhead lights had been left on. By their pale light he could make out the door to the supply closet. It was unlocked, as expected. He turned the knob and took a step into the room, only to stop abruptly as he realized that something was wrong. The light was on, which it should not have been.

But more than that, his razor-sharp instincts warned him that he was not alone.

His response was immediate as automatic reflexes took over. He threw his weight against the door, forcing it all the way open, and pushed past it instantly

into the closet. Even as he did so, one hand was
reaching inside his jacket for the Beretta, while the
other was closing on the throat of the person who had
been lying in wait for him.

Only when his fingers were digging into meltingly
soft skin did the image transmitted through his reti-
nas register on his brain and achieve recognition.

"Mollie."

Caught in the crook of his arm, pressed against his
unyielding chest, she was barely able to breathe. Her
eyes, wide as a frightened doe's, met his. His grip
eased, his hand falling away from her throat, though
he did not release her entirely.

Gingerly she touched the marks his fingers had left
as she croaked, "We have to stop meeting like this."

"I'm sorry...." The first shock of finding her there
had passed, at least enough for him to recollect himself. More firmly, he demanded, "What the hell are
you doing here?"

She swallowed, and was relieved to encounter little
difficulty. Her voice was stronger as she said, "Waiting for you, of course. You didn't really expect me to
fall for that business about picking me up at my
apartment."

As a matter of fact, she almost had. Only gradually
had it dawned on her that he might not stick to the
plan, and even then she had been loathe to believe it.
Rationalizing that if he went to her apartment and
didn't find her, he would go on to the tunnel, she had

decided it would do no harm to meet him there. Now she had to wonder about that.

Pointedly, she stared at the gun he still held. "I suppose next you'll be telling me that's standard issue for all history professors."

Sebastian sighed and belatedly put the Beretta away. He was making elementary mistakes, errors he hadn't committed since his training days, and he could only suppose that it was because she got to him in a way no one else ever had. Concerned as he was, it still amused him to see that she had taken his advice about clothes to heart.

Her jeans and shirt were a far cry from the elegant outfit she had worn earlier, but in their own way they were no less effective. If she had intended to disguise her long, slender legs with the soft, well-washed denim, she had failed, nor did the cotton shirt hide the full curves of her breasts. She had pulled her hair back in a ponytail, but loose tendrils curled around her forehead. She looked young, innocent and utterly desirable.

"Has anyone ever suggested to you," he asked laconically, "that you may need a keeper?"

"Certainly not. I'm perfectly capable of taking care of myself." At his frankly skeptical look, she shrugged. "Believe what you want, but don't make the mistake again of underestimating me. I may not be from the same background as you, but that doesn't mean I'm stupid."

"You know nothing about my background," he said softly.

"Don't I?" The look she shot him was gently perceptive. "I can make a few educated guesses, Professor."

The slightly mocking use of his title prepared him for what followed.

"You carry a very professional looking gun and seem to know how to use it. You know how to disable a person without causing serious injury, but I have the feeling that you could do much more if you chose. You reveal very little of yourself, which suggests that you have a great deal to hide. And, to top it all off, you are clearly concerned about keeping your presence here a secret, which leads me to wonder exactly what it is you're looking for."

She smiled faintly. "I've heard of academic rivalries, but I can't help but think that there's more to this than that."

There were people at the organization who would have hired her in a split second if they had heard her dissection of his cover story. She had cut right through it, peeling away all the carefully arranged layers of subterfuge to get to the very heart of the matter. Clearly, nothing less than the truth would satisfy her, but he was in no position to reveal it, at least not entirely.

"All right," he said after a long moment. "Let's quit playing games with each other. There is more involved than an interesting historical find, but I can't tell you what it is. If you have any sense, you'll accept that and go away."

"Is that what you want?"

He looked into her bright eyes, where green and gold mingled as if in a sun-drenched forest. He thought about how beautiful she was, how strong and yielding, how she made him feel things he never had before.

She was so far beyond the life he had chosen; yet she also represented everything he fought for. All that was good and enduring, all that most deserved protecting. All those thoughts were in his mind as he met her gaze and nodded. "Yes, I want you to leave."

Mollie swallowed the stab of hurt, telling herself that she shouldn't be surprised at anything he said or did. There was far more involved here than she could guess, but she was still determined to see it through.

"Sorry, I have no intention of bowing out. Whatever's in that tunnel, I mean to help you find it." Especially since the alternative apparently was for him to go down alone, the mere thought of which made her feel sick inside.

"Mollie . . ." Softly, he reached out to her, the back of his hand brushing her cheek. "It could be dangerous."

She struggled to ignore the tingling caused by his touch. "Because of the rats?"

"Of all kinds. Give it up, Mollie." She couldn't know how much those words cost him; the urge to cling to her, to let her wipe away all the loneliness and danger, almost overwhelmed him.

Before its onrushing force, he might have felt less than a man, but instead his masculinity was stronger than ever. It took strength to admit his need for her, even if he wouldn't acknowledge it out loud.

The tiny spurt of relief he felt when she shook her head was instantly forced down. He managed to frown as she said, "Nice try, Sebastian, but it won't work. I'm going with you, or I'm going alone. You pick."

"That's a hell of a choice."

Her only response was to turn toward the back wall and begin removing the supplies on the shelves. He muttered something under his breath and set to work helping her.

"Shut the door," he directed when they were ready to shift the wall. As she did so, he lifted the plasterboard and carefully set it to one side.

"How did you find out about this?" Mollie asked.

"By studying the plans of this building, then matching them to the plans of the older structure, which are still in the city archives."

"The tunnel was on the plans?" That didn't seem very likely to her, not if it had been built for the purpose she presumed.

He sighed, wondering if she would ever accept anything he said at face value without probing more deeply and catching him out. "No," he admitted, " we learned of the tunnel from another source."

Before she could ask anything further, he said firmly, "And that's all I'm going to tell you. Let's get on with it."

Reluctantly, she agreed. Much as she wanted to know the identity of the "we" he referred to and the details of how they had discovered the tunnel, she was more eager to discover what might be in it. Visions of a chest of antique coins or some other treasure flitted through her mind as she followed him down the stone steps.

It was cold in the tunnel. The beam of light he shone revealed moisture dripping down the dank walls. The scurrying sound she had noticed the first time seemed even more evident now. Instinctively she flinched, trying not to think about what might be under her feet.

"Having fun?" he demanded caustically before they had gone very far.

"Tons. When do you think this was built, anyway?"

"Sometime in the 1770's," he told her grudgingly, "when the British were cracking down on imports to the Colonies, imposing all sorts of taxes."

"The kind that led to the Boston Tea Party?"

"About the same. They made the same mistakes over and over, and the people inevitably found a way around them."

"Including smuggling?" She was genuinely interested, but she also realized that she wanted to keep him talking to allay her own nervousness. Even if he were only tolerating her presence, his voice had an oddly soothing effect.

"Especially. It became the lifeblood of the Colonies and the early Republic." He broke off suddenly. "Watch your step here; the stone is crumbling."

Mollie did as he said, aware that they had penetrated much farther into the tunnel than she had managed originally. Air, heavy with smells she couldn't identify, moved over her. She shivered and wrapped her arms around herself. "I didn't think it could go very far from the building," she murmured.

"The main tunnel ends about half a block from here. It runs into the foundation of the World Trade Center. But there are branch tunnels that need to be checked."

"Are there many of them?" Even to her own ears, her voice sounded tremulous.

Sebastian turned to look at her. In the pale beam of light, her face looked white, her eyes unnaturally wide and dark. "Are you okay?"

His gruff concern embarrassed her. She had pulled out all the stops to come along; it was ridiculous to be acting like a frightened child. "Of course. It's probably safer down here than on the streets up above."

"Maybe," he said, without conviction. "Just remember that you know your way around up there and you don't down here. If you've got any ideas about wandering off on your own . . ."

"I don't," Mollie assured him. She would have to be crazy to do that, when right now the only security she had was in the tall, powerful form so close beside her. "But it might help if you'd give me a better idea of what we're looking for."

"I'm not sure, exactly," he admitted. "It might be something as obvious as a small case or trunk, or it might be as hard to spot as a loose stone in these walls that could be hiding a recess of some kind."

"So whatever we're after, it's been here a long time?"

"If it's here at all."

"And whatever it is, someone else wants it."

"I didn't say that," Sebastian protested. He had stopped abruptly, and she came smack up against the solid wall of his back.

"You did everything but," Mollie muttered, taking a quick step back. Each time she touched him, even accidentally, she was made vividly aware of the tensile strength of his body, the tightly coiled power waiting to be unleashed.

Deliberately seeking a lighter note, she said, "Let's see if I can guess. Someone hid the property deed to all of Manhattan down here, and whoever finds it owns the whole shebang. How's that sound?"

"Terrific; it would make this the ultimate treasure hunt. But unfortunately, you're wrong."

"Am I at least close?"

He smiled lightly. "Close doesn't count."

"That's a lousy attitude. I should at least get points for trying."

"Yes," he agreed gently, "you should, but it doesn't work that way in real life. Nobody gives you points for anything except winning."

"Is that what you teach your students?"

He relented slightly in the face of her obvious dismay and shook his head. "No, I teach them about the struggle and sacrifice that created our country, and, I hope, I encourage them to make their own contribution."

"Is that what you're doing," she asked softly. "Making a contribution?"

He looked at her directly for an instant, and in his eyes she saw something she had never expected to see: a hint of vulnerability, of a need for understanding and acceptance that made her want to reach out to him. It was gone almost before she could be sure her mind hadn't been playing tricks on her, and in its place was the cool self-possession she had already come to associate with him.

"If you like." They had entered one of the branches of the tunnel. Mollie could make out a door at the far end.

"Look," she said excitedly, "another entrance."

"I checked it last time. It's sealed over."

"Oh." Her initial disappointment faded as she noticed something unusual about the wall near where they were standing. "Have you seen what's over here?" she asked, leaning closer to get a better look. "People have carved their initials."

"Graffiti goes way back. It's even been found in ancient Pompeii."

"And in the cliffs where the Egyptian pharaohs were buried. Isn't it fascinating, though, to think of the people who actually stood where we are now? If you shut your eyes, you can almost see them."

"I prefer to keep mine open," he said dryly, yet he shared her enthusiasm. Those moments when history came alive were the source of its fascination.

She shot him a chiding glance and continued her perusal of the stone. "Look at this one. Ichabod Bradford, 7 August 1779. You were right, the tunnel was in use during the Revolution."

"Let me see that." Sebastian pushed her gently aside as he shone the flashlight on the faint carving. He touched the surface of the stone carefully, his long fingers feeling around the mortar that held it in place. "It's loose."

"After all these years, that can't be unusual." She tried to keep the rising tide of excitement under control, but the sudden urgency she sensed in Sebastian made that very difficult.

"Not like this. It feels as though the stone was never actually mortared into the wall, just placed within it." He handed her the flashlight. "Here, hold this."

She did as he said, training the beam on the stone as he slowly eased it from the wall. Behind it she could make out a small recess. "We've found it," Mollie said delightedly.

"Maybe, maybe not." Sebastian peered into the hole. It was about eight inches high and a foot wide, and deep enough that he could not see the back of it. Cautiously, he stuck his hand in and began to feel around. "Someone did a good job on this. We might never have found it if you hadn't noticed the graffiti."

"Do you think Ichabod Bradford might have marked it deliberately?"

"Could be. He was a Revolutionary patriot, fought in the War of Independence as a young man and served again as an officer in the War of 1812. In between, he ran a very successful business in New York, not far from here."

"So he could have been familiar with the tunnel?"

"It seems he definitely was, but..." His hand emerged, empty. "Whatever he put in here is gone." Sebastian brushed stone dust from his fingers and took the flashlight back from her.

He smiled gently at her disappointment even as he struggled to mask his own. Finding the empty cache wasn't necessarily a bad sign; on the other hand, it wasn't a good one, either.

"We'll have to keep looking, but before we do, let's get some fresh air."

Mollie nodded. The air in the tunnel was stale; after even a few minutes of breathing it she heard a faint ringing in her ears.

They walked back along the way they had come and up the stone steps. Sebastian went to open the door. She heard him mutter something under his breath.

"What's wrong?" she asked.

"It won't open." He pushed again, without any effect.

"I don't understand.... It opened fine before."

"But it doesn't now." He leaned his shoulders against the door and let it have his full weight. Nothing happened. "Something's barring it." Under his breath, he cursed. He should have anticipated this and taken steps to prevent it, but that hindsight would do them no good. He would be better off concentrating on who had blocked the door, and why.

At least Mollie was staying calm. A glance at her reassured him that she had a good grip on herself. Either that, or the meaning of the situation hadn't fully sunk in to her yet.

In fact, it had, and she was having to concentrate all her energies on not giving in to panic. The darkness seemed to press in on them despite the thin beam from the flashlight.

She felt the damp coldness clear through to her bones. The stale air, fetid smells and ominous sounds made her tremble. For the first time, she understood what it must mean to be claustrophobic.

"Sebastian . . . we will get out of here, won't we?"

He was studying the door again and didn't answer at once, not until the slightly thin, high sound of her

voice registered with him. Then he straightened up and
turned to her.

"You're not scared, are you?"

His faintly mocking tone was the challenge she
needed. Stiffening her shoulders, she said, "Of course
not. I just thought it would be rather boring if we were
stuck down here all night."

"Boring? No," he said more softly, "I'm afraid the
last thing it's going to be is boring."

Chapter 6

There's another way out," Sebastian said. Before Mollie could give vent to her immense relief, he went on. "But it's tricky to get to, and there may be a problem."

"What sort of problem?" Whatever it was, she was sure they could deal with it. All that really mattered was that they weren't trapped.

"We may have...company." He paused, debating how much to tell her, finally deciding that she had a right to know what they were up against. "I think someone locked us in here deliberately, and that those same people may want to stop us from finding whatever's in the tunnel."

"Then they're in for a disappointment. This is just a little inconvenience."

"Mollie..." Rather to his own surprise, he reached out and took her hand, holding it gently. "These aren't very nice people we're dealing with. They'll use any methods they have to in order to get what they want."

Her eyes widened as she took in the full import of his words. "Oh...then I was right about this not being simply a matter of academic rivalry?"

"Unfortunately not. I should never have allowed you to become involved. Whatever happens, I hope you'll forgive me for that."

His genuine remorse took her aback. The situation must be even worse than she thought to make him look so grim. "I seem to remember," she said quietly, "that it was my decision to come along."

"But my responsibility."

"No," she corrected him. "I'm a grown woman, Sebastian, responsible for myself. Besides," she added more lightly, "whoever these bad guys are, they don't realize what they're tangling with. You should actually feel sorry for them."

The corners of his mouth quirked. Inwardly he applauded her courage even as he hoped it wouldn't really be needed. "I hadn't thought of it that way."

Keeping a firm hold on her hand, he started back down the stairs. At the bottom, he turned off the flashlight and said softly, "Let's give our eyes a chance to adjust to the dark."

She didn't ask why he was reluctant to use the flashlight. Remembering how it had caused her to spot

him the first time, she realized that it could give away
their location to whoever else might be in the tunnel.

"Keep behind me," he whispered after several moments. "Don't make any more noise than you can
help, and be prepared to do exactly what I tell you."

She nodded, glad that she didn't have to talk anymore, since the tightness of her throat made it all but
impossible. Instead, she concentrated on taking long,
steady breaths that she hoped would calm her.

They had gone the equivalent of a couple of blocks
when Sebastian suddenly said, "Get back against the
wall."

She obeyed instantly, pressing herself against the
clammy stones. Sebastian was very close, sheltering
her with his body. She saw the glint of dark metal as
he pulled out the gun, heard the trigger click as it was
cocked.

"Wh-what . . ." she began.

"Quiet."

A shot rang out. Mollie flinched as shards of stone
exploded directly beside her head. Terror gripped her.
She started to scream but had no breath for it. Her
heart pounded against her ribs, and her stomach
clenched sickeningly.

Everything seemed to be happening in slow motion. Sebastian pushed her onto the ground and came
down beside her. She could feel the hardness of the
stone pressing into her hips and thighs, the moisture
seeping through her clothes. He was a shadow in the
darkness, his arms stretched out in front of him, el-

bows bent, the gun glinting in his hands. She watched, riveted, as he lifted his head, took careful aim and fired.

The flare of light from the muzzle of the gun made her momentarily close her eyes. They sprang open an instant later when he gripped her arm as he surged to his feet, pulling her with him.

"Come on." Together they dashed across the tunnel. Shots rang out around them, seeming to come from several directions. Sebastian shoved her against the wall and turned to fire again.

There was a muffled groan and the sound of a body falling heavily, then silence. They ran again, moving to a different part of the tunnel. He put a finger to his lips, cautioning her not to speak. Any sound, however faint, might give away their new position.

She leaned her head back against the wall, struggling against the nausea that burned her throat. Never could she have imagined herself in such a situation. Not all the shoot-outs she had seen on television or read of in books had prepared her for the real thing. Terror gnawed at her insides, mocking her with her frantic desire to live.

It wasn't simply a matter of someone trying to scare them off; they were the quarry in a deadly game of cat and mouse. That much she understood without having to be told. What she wasn't sure of was whether the game was still on, or Sebastian had put a lethal end to it.

That he had shot to kill she did not doubt. She had seen the cold, implacable glint in his eye as he took aim. He was no stranger to violence, and he did not hesitate to use it for his own ends.

But had he succeeded? There was only one way to find out, and she had to stand by and watch him take it.

Slowly, with all his senses keenly alert, Sebastian looked around the corner into the main tunnel. He could see little and knew that he himself would be only a faint blur of motion against the darkness. But that would be enough if, as he suspected, a second killer lurked in wait.

In his experience, terrorists rarely worked alone, whether because they didn't trust each other or because they simply preferred to tip the odds in their favor didn't really matter. There was always a backup to finish the mission if the first attempt failed.

Because he knew this, the next shot did not take him by surprise. He pulled back even as it fractured the rock in front of him. Mollie made a strangled sound deep in her throat. He pressed a hard hand to her mouth and thrust her deeper into the tunnel.

"Stay here," he whispered in her ear. "Don't move until I tell you." He presumed that he would be around to do so. He didn't care to consider the alternative—for either of them.

She nodded mutely, her eyes holding his for a moment before he tore his gaze away. Soundlessly, like a great hunting cat, he moved back down the tunnel, gun at the ready. When he reached the corner, he stopped and crouched low near the floor. He drew a breath deep enough to fill his lungs, then held it.

In the absolute silence, he could hear only the rush of his blood in his ears and the drip of water down the walls. Mollie was utterly still behind him, not moving an inch. He gave silent thanks for her strength as he projected all his senses forward, into the darkness that hid the enemy.

Slowly, beginning as barely an inkling on the edge of his brain, he caught a sense of movement. Still not breathing, he waited...waited...waited...until the faintest disruption in the pattern of darkness told him what he needed to know.

He came out of the crouch fluidly, the gun raised, and fired in the same instant that he hurled himself across the tunnel, almost—but not quite—quickly enough. His bullet found its target, and there was another muffled scream, but not before the second assailant got off a round of his own. That bullet struck the wall behind Sebastian and ricochetted off, gashing his forehead and making him reel backward.

Pinwheels of lights swam before his eyes. He put a hand to his hairline and felt the stickiness of blood. His heart was hammering painfully in his chest, and his pulse beat erratically, both signals that he was going into shock.

Even as he fought to hold onto consciousness, he could feel it slipping away from him. His last thought was to try to reach Mollie, to at least give her the gun, but before he could do so his knees buckled and he slid soundlessly to the ground.

Mollie had not moved. She remained frozen in place where Sebastian had left her. Frantically, she waited for him to return. When he did not, she wondered desperately what to do.

He had said to stay where she was, but how could she do that, not knowing what had happened to him? He might be simply trying to lull their assailants into revealing themselves, or he might have been hurt. Perhaps even worse.

That didn't bear thinking about. She took a deep breath, uttered a silent prayer, and took a step forward. When nothing happened, she dared another and another, until finally she came to the corner leading into the main tunnel.

A dark shape was slumped on the other side. Sebastian? Hesitantly, she called his name. When there was no answer, she tried again more loudly. Her voice, low as it was, seemed to reverberate in the tunnel. She shrank back, expecting immediate discovery.

Moments passed, and nothing happened. Cautiously, she crept forward until she could kneel beside the huddled form and gingerly turn it over.

Sebastian. Breath rushed from her in a soft hiss. She could see the trickle of blood on his forehead and knew an agonizing stab of dread, but the slow rise and fall of his chest reassured her.

Several years before Mollie had taken a first aid course; now it served her well. She was able to find his pulse and determine that it was slow but steady. Whatever had happened to him, the effects were at least lessening.

Gently, she propped him up and called his name softly. "Sebastian, can you hear me? You have to wake up. We can't stay here, and I can't carry you."

Repeatedly she spoke to him, until finally she was rewarded with a slight flicker of his eyelids. Slowly they opened, and he gazed at her, at first uncomprehendingly.

"It's Mollie. You've been shot, but I don't think it's too serious. We have to get out of here."

Comprehension dawned. He started to nod, caught himself as pain lanced through him, and managed to smile faintly. "Feels like a building fell on me."

She grimaced sympathetically. "Can you stand?"

"I think so...." With her help, he was able to make it to his feet. His arm was draped over her shoulder as she tried to take as much of his weight as she could bear. He kept the gun in his free hand, ready to use it, even though he wasn't sure how steady his aim would be.

"Do you want to go back and try the door again?" she asked.

"There's no point. We'll have to find the other way out." He took a deep breath, fighting a wave of dizziness. "It should be in that direction."

Mollie peered down the tunnel. It was completely dark, and there was no sign of any movement. Slowly, they started forward.

Before they had gone very far, they found the first body. Mollie cried out softly and tried to pull back, but Sebastian would not let her. "Don't look at it," he ordered even as he took a quick glance himself to make sure the man was dead. He could feel Mollie trembling against him and was grateful that she said nothing.

The second man lay a little further on, also dead. This time Mollie made no effort to pull away, only averted her head and kept going. Sebastian's admiration for her increased even further. He had known few women with such courage, and fewer still who also possessed a full complement of human emotions. In fact, he could think of no one with whom to compare Mollie.

Such thoughts would do him no good, not when he had to concentrate all his attention on getting them out of the tunnel safely. "Through there," he directed, pointing toward another branch. "This part of the tunnel runs parallel to the subway tracks. There's an opening that should be large enough for us to get through." At least he hoped it would be.

They felt the vibration of a train a short time later and almost immediately saw a flicker of light. The opening was near the roof of the tunnel, where several stones had fallen away. Mollie looked at it dubiously, wondering how they would be able to reach it, let alone get through to the other side.

"I'll give you a boost," Sebastian said.

Immediately she thought of his wound. "You're not strong enough."

He smiled faintly. "You don't think so? Let's find out."

She wanted to protest but, realizing that there was no other way, reluctantly agreed. He bent down slightly and laced his fingers together to form a step, grimacing as he did so. "Put your foot in there and hold onto my shoulders."

She did as he said, stifling a gasp when he boosted her upward, high enough so that she could get a handhold on the crumbled stone. "Ease your shoulders through first," he instructed through gritted teeth. Ordinarily he would have had no difficulty with her weight, but the effects of his wound had weakened him. His legs trembled as he forced himself to lift her further.

"I can make it through," Mollie called, her voice muffled. "It's not much of a drop on the other side." She pulled herself upward, wincing as her arms and legs scraped against the sharp rock. With difficulty, she managed to twist around so that she could fall feet first.

"All right?" Sebastian called when he heard her land on the other side.

"Yes, but what about you?"

Good question. He could hear the anxiousness in her voice and knew she was worried about his ability to make it through. But then, she didn't know how many times he'd been in tighter spots.

Several deep, controlled breaths boosted his strength to the maximum possible under the circumstances. His head throbbed, but he ignored it as he scanned the wall, looking for footholds. Finding them, he began to climb and quickly reached the opening.

His shoulders were almost too broad to fit through. He had to twist them sharply. The stones tore at his chest and arms, though the tightly woven material of his clothes did not rip. He would have abrasions and bruises, but nothing more serious.

Mollie's face was white and strained when he finally dropped down beside her. She looked at the fresh blood trickling down his forehead and swallowed hard. "Are you all right?"

"Fine," he assured her, though he was anything but. The wound was deeper than he had thought at first. He couldn't count on being on his feet much longer.

"Let's get our bearings and keep moving," he said quietly. They were standing at the far end of a subway platform. There were no lights where they were, since only workman normally came here, and they were off until the following day. In the distance, they could see a handful of people waiting for the next train.

Mollie and Sebastian walked past them quickly. They drew a few curious looks, but those were hastily averted. New Yorkers knew better than to make eye contact with anyone who might be even potentially dangerous.

Moments later they had climbed the stairs from the platform and were outside in the fresh night air. After the staleness of the tunnel, it was very welcome. They both took deep, reviving breaths as they glanced around.

"My car is parked near here," Sebastian said. He was having difficulty speaking clearly, and everything had begun to look slightly out of focus. "I think you'd better drive."

She agreed without question. One glance at him was enough to tell her that he was in bad shape. "You need a doctor. There's a hospital not far from here."

"No," he said flatly. "We'll go to my apartment, and then I'll find some way to get you home."

Mollie bit her lip and said nothing further. He would find out soon enough that she had no intention of leaving him. She had never driven a car as expensive as his Jaguar and was terrified of doing something to it, but he didn't seem to be at all concerned. Normally, perhaps he would have been. As it was, he sat with his head back and his eyes closed, and said nothing.

She found the address he had given her without difficulty and pulled into the underground garage. On their way up to his apartment, they encountered no one.

"I'll call you a taxi," Sebastian said as he unlocked the door and reached inside to disarm the security system. He did so with difficulty, his head swimming as he struggled to remember the combination.

"I can get one later," Mollie told him. "First, I want to make sure you're all right."

He shook his head, immediately regretting doing so. "There's no need. I appreciate your help, but it would be best for you to leave now." He had to get her out of there before he could call headquarters and report what had happened.

"I don't think so," Mollie said as she stepped into the living room. Its hominess surprised her. Instead of the stark, modern furniture she had expected, there were comfortable couches and tables, a lovely Oriental rug, and a fireplace that looked well used. One entire wall was lined with books, which she longed to examine at a more opportune time.

"A doctor really has to look at that wound," she said as she turned back to Sebastian. He was still standing in the entry hall, watching her.

"Yes, I know. About that cab..."

"Forget it. I told you, I'm not leaving until I'm sure you're all right."

"That's very nice of you, but—"

"No buts. I realize you want me to leave, but I won't. You'll just have to accept that." She faced him defiantly, daring him to try to force her to leave. Her own determination surprised her; normally she would never have been so rude as to insist on remaining where she was not welcome. It was only the conviction that Sebastian really did not want to be left alone that made her insist on staying.

"You're being very stubborn," he said, swaying slightly. Instantly, she was at his side, helping him to sit down.

"Where's the bathroom?" she asked. "I want to get a wet cloth for your forehead."

He told her, then waited until she was gone before getting to his feet again. He intended to make the call before she returned, but his uncertain balance and the buzzing in his ears prevented him from reaching the phone in time.

She found him halfway across the room, leaning against the wall. "*I'm* stubborn? You take the cake. Can't you sit still for a minute?" As she spoke, she eased under his arm and helped him back to the couch.

"Hold still," she directed. "I want to see how bad this is."

Sebastian did not move as she gently wiped away the dry blood, but Mollie flinched at what lay beneath. The wound was deep and ragged; if the angle had been even slightly different, the bullet would have entered his brain. She cringed at the thought even as she fought to keep her voice steady. "We should have gone to the hospital. Now we'll have to go anyway."

"No," he said firmly. At her mutinous look, he added, "There's someone I can call, if you wouldn't mind bringing me the phone."

She did so reluctantly, since she doubted that any doctor would come out in the middle of the night to tend to such an injury, not when it could be better seen to in an emergency room.

Her back stiffened as she heard what Sebastian was saying. "This is Eagle. I need assistance. Cleanup at the site and medical here. A flesh wound to the forehead." He was silent for a moment, listening to someone on the other end, then hung up and met her bewildered gaze.

"They'll be here in five minutes. I want you to leave."

"No." How could she, when she was more curious than ever. Why was he called "Eagle?" Who had he called? Were the police to be kept out of it, and if so, how?

"You don't understand," he began. "I don't want you to be involved."

Her eyes met his with grave sincerity. "But I already am."

He started to speak, to try to convince her otherwise, but stopped when he realized that she was right: she was involved. Harder to admit, but nonetheless true, was the fact that he wanted it that way.

After so many years of being alone, fighting battles other men would have run from, he was tired and dispirited. Something deep within him cried out for her warmth and gentleness. Even as he told himself he would regret it, he closed his eyes and accepted what was to be.

Chapter 7

Several hours later, the first gray light of dawn was beginning to chase the shadows from the sky. Pigeons rose on fluttering wings from the caverns between buildings. Off in the distance, Mollie could hear the lonely call of a ship's whistle on the river.

She was very tired. Her eyes burned, and the effort to keep her lids open seemed to require all her concentration, yet she was determined to stay awake, at least until she was really sure that Sebastian was all right.

He slept deeply, and seemingly without dreams. She could see the steady rise and fall of his chest beneath the sheet, and was comforted by it.

The doctor had been a surprise, but then, so had almost everything else that had happened that night.

He had arrived as quickly as Sebastian had promised, a tall, thin man with a quiet manner and sharp eyes. Her presence must have required some explanation, but Sebastian had offered none, and she had taken the cue from him and kept silent.

The examination had been swift and to the point. "You were lucky," the doctor had said. "Another inch or so and it would have been a different story."

Sebastian hadn't commented. What was there, after all, for him to say? He was alive; his assailants were dead. Whatever compassion he might have felt for them was erased by the knowledge that they had not acted alone; the battle was far from over.

"I don't want those," he had said when the doctor shook out several small white pills.

"Suit yourself, but that head is going to hurt. I'd give you a shot right away, but you may have a concussion, so I can't risk it." He had glanced at Mollie. "Will you be around to keep an eye on him at least for the next few hours?"

"That isn't necessary," Sebastian had answered.

"Certainly," she had said.

The doctor had almost smiled, but caught himself in time. "Let me put it this way, somebody has to check on you while you're asleep to make sure you aren't slipping in to a coma. If the lady will do it, fine. Otherwise, I'm checking you into the clinic."

Sebastian had stayed there once before, when he was recovering from the injury that had left him scarred, and he had no wish to return to the organization's private medical facility. Though it was housed in a mansion near Princeton, New Jersey, surrounded by lush grounds and provided with every imaginable luxury, it had still felt like a prison to him.

Reluctantly, he had looked at Mollie. "If you wouldn't mind staying...?"

She had assured him that she did not, and the doctor had left shortly thereafter. Sebastian had grudgingly agreed to get into bed. When she had offered to get his pajamas he had curtly informed her that he didn't wear any, and if her modesty were liable to be offended, she should absent herself until he was safely under the covers.

She had settled for turning her back, glad that he couldn't see her flaming cheeks as visions of him unclothed darted through her mind. When she had looked again, he was stretched out on the bed, the sheet pulled up to his waist, revealing his broad chest lightly sprinkled with hair.

"You don't really have to stay," he had insisted.

"I told the doctor I would." Before he could object further, she had turned off the light and sat down in a chair near the bed.

"Mollie..."

"Yes?"

"Thank you." The words were so softly uttered that she barely heard them, but when she did, she smiled.

Periodically throughout the night she had awakened him, as the doctor had instructed, making sure that he was fully conscious. Each time he slipped swiftly back into sleep. Watching him, she noted how the hard lines in his face relaxed, and imagined that she was seeing him as he must have been years ago, before time and experience etched their marks on him.

Curled up in the chair, covered by an afghan she had found in a chest at the foot of the bed, she struggled to stay awake. But at length her head fell forward, her bright auburn hair a curtain hiding her face, and she, too, slept.

Sebastian turned over and murmured to himself. He was rising through successive layers of consciousness, shedding the deep cloak of sleep that had restored his strength. Vaguely he remembered Mollie waking him, recalled the concern in her eyes and the gentleness of her touch. He thought she must have been a dream, until he opened his eyes and saw her.

She was asleep in the chair, her legs drawn under her and the afghan pulled up to her chin. The hair spilling across her face was a veil he longed to part. He wanted to see and touch her, to hear her voice again and be sure that she wasn't simply a figment of his imagination.

Instead, he let her sleep and moved soundlessly from the bed, pausing only to pick up clean clothes. In the bathroom, he showered and shaved, grimacing at the unnatural paleness of his features. He touched the bandage on his forehead and was satisfied when the wound hurt only slightly. The doctor had, as usual, done a thorough job.

Mollie was still asleep when he slipped through the bedroom on his way to the kitchen. He put coffee on and found a package of frozen croissants that he stuck in the microwave. When the impromptu breakfast was ready, he carried it on a tray back to the bedroom and gently woke her.

"Mollie...it's time to get up. You can't be very comfortable like that."

She stirred reluctantly and opened her eyes, meeting his. "Sebastian?" A slender hand brushed aside the heavy weight of her hair. "Are you all right?"

"Fine," he assured her. "Thanks to you. I really appreciate everything you did."

She shrugged that off and sat up straighter. "It was nothing. Is that coffee I smell?"

He nodded. "Hope you like it strong."

"This morning I do." She accepted a cup gratefully and stretched to try to unkink her muscles.

"That chair wasn't made for sleeping in," he said apologetically. "You really should have taken the couch, or, better yet, shared the bed."

She took a sip of the rather bitter coffee before replying. "The couch was too far away, and I didn't feel comfortable sharing a bed with you."

"Why not?" he asked, sitting down on the side of the bed facing her.

"Because you had made it clear that you didn't want me here." That wasn't the complete explanation, but it would do.

He sighed deeply and ran a hand through his rumpled hair. "I did give you that impression, didn't I?" When she nodded, he went on. "Incorrectly, of course. The last thing I wanted was for you to leave."

"Then why did you tell me to?"

"Because I also didn't want you to become any more involved than you already were. There are . . . problems you don't know about."

"Actually," she said quietly, "I think I've pretty well got it figured out. As I mentioned earlier, you're not at all the typical history professor."

"And here I've tried so hard to be convincing," he protested wryly. "Would it make any difference to tell you that I really do have a Ph.D. from Harvard in American history and have been teaching that subject for almost ten years?"

"I don't doubt it," she said serenely. "What interests me, though, is what you're up to when you aren't in the classroom. You obviously have, shall we say, a wide range of skills."

She took another sip of the coffee and accepted a croissant from the basket he held out. With it came a fresh linen napkin, a small dish filled with blackberry jam, and a delicate porcelain plate.

Mollie shook her head in admiration. "You really are very domesticated."

"Has it occurred to you that I might be gay?"

She choked on her croissant and swallowed hastily. "No," she lied. "Are you?"

"'Fraid not. Maybe it would be better if I were."

"Why?"

"Because then I wouldn't feel the way I do about you. I'd have enough sense to send you packing."

A speck of the blackberry jam had lodged in the corner of Mollie's mouth. She licked it away absently as she stared at him. "Should I take that to mean you feel some . . . attraction toward me?"

Sebastian followed the motion of her tongue with narrowed eyes. He shifted on the bed. "You could say that."

"Oh . . ." Their heads were very close. She could see the silver glints in his eyes and the deep, glossy brown of his hair. Small lines marked the corners of his slightly full mouth. She watched, fascinated, as his lips parted, revealing even white teeth.

Gently, he reached out and took the delicate china cup and plate from her, setting them on the bedside table. With equal gentleness, his hand slipped beneath her hair, coming to rest on the nape of her neck.

"You are a lovely woman, Mollie," he murmured, pressing ever so slightly so that she leaned toward him. "If I had any sense, I'd hustle you out of here before your feet could touch the ground."

"Why don't you?" she asked, barely breathing. She could smell the warmth of him, taste the mingled scents of soap and musk clinging to his skin. The tips of her fingers tingled with the urge to touch him, to learn for herself the planes and angles of his lean, hard body.

"Because..." he said deep in his throat, "of this." His mouth closed over hers, parting her lips with remorseless ease. He did not coax or plead, but simply took what he already regarded as his own. Only then did he begin to suspect how much he was also giving of himself.

Mollie's eyes fluttered shut. Thick auburn lashes cast dark shadows on her cheeks. She felt a sudden heaviness in her breasts and between her thighs, as though all her life force was concentrating in those especially female places. The sensation shocked her. She opened her eyes again and tried to move away.

Reflexively, Sebastian stopped her. He sensed the surprise and fear coursing through her and knew it was directed not at him but at herself. If he let her draw back now, neither of them would be served.

"Sweet...Mollie...let me..." He soothed her with the low, caressing sound of his voice, the gentle touch of his hands, the softening brush of his mouth.

The tremulous flutters of apprehension died within her, replaced by a burgeoning sense of fullness, almost as though a tight bud was unfurling petal by petal inside her.

His tongue touched lightly against the barrier of her teeth, coaxing them apart. The warm, velvet touch of him drove her to reciprocate. Lightly they feinted and parried, drawing each other out, playing lovers' games until both were tense with need and breathlessness.

Sebastian called a halt first. He leaned back, his lean cheeks flushed, and smiled tenderly. "Mollie, my dear, if I had the brains of a gnat, I'd be scared to death of you."

Her eyebrows rose provocatively. "I could say the same about myself."

He threw back his head and laughed for the pure joy of her honesty. "Don't you know you're supposed to be coquettishly coy?"

Mollie tried that out, but had trouble even saying it. "Too alliterative. Besides, all I really know how to be is me." She looked up at him through the thick fringe of her lashes. "I'm afraid that will just have to do."

"Oh, Lord," Sebastian said under his breath as he met her gaze, "I really am sunk."

For a man who felt as though he were going down for the third time, he was downright cheerful. After breakfast, which included good-natured teasing about the number of crumbs on the bed and her intention to teach him how to make proper coffee, Mollie mentioned a desire to return to her own apartment to freshen up.

"While I'm at it," she said reluctantly, "I suppose I really should go in to work."

"Let's spend the day together instead. That is, if you aren't too tired." He realized that she must have had very little sleep, and that only in a chair.

Mollie might have expected to feel worn out, but there was something about being with him that banished any sense of fatigue. Instead she felt wide awake and excited at the prospect of a day with him. "You talked me into it."

Mindful of how heavy traffic was at that hour of the morning, they took a cab to Mollie's apartment in SoHo. She had moved there right out of college, just before the neighborhood of spacious lofts and artists' studios had become fashionable.

Six months before, her building, an old brick warehouse, had gone condominium, and she had taken advantage of her right as a resident to buy at a bargain price. Since then, she'd been offered a considerable profit if she would sell, but had steadfastly refused.

Her apartment took up a good part of the top floor. Reached by a rickety service elevator, it comprised more than a thousand feet of living space left completely open except for a closed-in central area that held the kitchen and bath.

Large windows faced south, admitting a steady supply of sunlight to nourish the tree-sized plants she had scattered about. The furniture was minimal—a few good kilim rugs, modular seating units, half a dozen large needlepoint pillows she had done herself. One entire wall was given over to bookcases that held most of her library; the rest of the books were in closets, out of sight.

In the midst of all this homey splendor, the cat Mehitabel lounged Sphinxlike, observing their arrival with unblinking eyes.

"She's annoyed at me for not coming home last night," Mollie said as she picked the ginger feline up and scratched her apologetically behind the ear.

Mehitabel ignored her, preferring to concentrate on Sebastian, who returned her gaze unflinchingly. Man and cat assessed each other until each was satisfied.

"Oomph." Mehitabel's back paws pushed into Mollie's stomach as she jumped down and strolled off to the kitchen. "I guess she's all right." Without the cat to distract her, she felt suddenly self-conscious. "I'll get changed."

"Mind if I make more coffee?"

"Of course not. Make yourself..." She almost said "at home," thought better of it and settled for "comfortable."

The kitchen was small but well-organized. Fresh daffodils sat in a brown pottery jug on the tiled counter. Copper pots hanging from an overhead rack gleamed brightly. A note stuck to the refrigerator said "Don't forget to buy milk." Sebastian smiled to himself.

He nodded politely to Mehitabel, who was stretched out on top of one of the oak cabinets watching him. "Where's the coffee pot?"

The merest flicker of a tail tip drew his glance to a prettily quilted cover, which, when removed, revealed an automatic coffee maker. Coincidence? He supposed so, but looked at Mehitabel with new respect.

While the coffee was brewing, he wandered out into the main seating area and looked around. The first impression, so pleasing to his esthetic sensibilities, held up well on further examination. Each object had clearly been chosen with care, not from any desire to impress but simply to create an atmosphere conducive to relaxation.

He could get very used to being here. Something was happening to him that he couldn't define and that was outside of all his experience. He was being made aware of vague longings, nebulous discontents, a yearning for something he did not have.

Wryly, he wondered if perhaps he was simply getting old. Thirty-four was hardly ancient in most fields, but in his it signified long, often brutally hard, experience, which inevitably took its toll. He was a senior man in the organization, looked up to by the other, younger agents. That usually amused him, but just now it did not. It rankled to think that he might be over the hill when he felt at the peak of his mental and physical powers.

Certainly, if his reaction to Mollie was anything to go by, he was hardly old. His eyes narrowed speculatively as he remembered his response to her. When had he last felt such passion with a woman? Not in a very long time, if ever.

The coffee was ready. He went back into the kitchen and poured himself a cup. Mehitabel jumped down from the cabinet and brushed against him, purring softly.

"So you think I'm okay?" he asked, scratching her back. The only answer he received was a deeper purr, then a flick of her tail as she strolled away, but not without a backward glance.

Meanwhile Mollie was going through the motions of getting herself ready for the day. She had showered and washed her hair, then dried it as best she could given its weight and length, and her own disinclination to linger. It was still slightly damp when she pulled on a wraparound skirt and a T-shirt.

On the other side of the bathroom, open to the rest of the loft but with a sense of privacy, she had set up her big brass bed. Beside it, on a mahogany and marble Victorian nightstand, was the telephone. She put a call through to the office, explaining that she had decided to take another vacation day. That was no problem, since the first week of July was normally a slow time. Her conscience clear, she went to rejoin Sebastian.

They spent the morning wandering around SoHo—so named because it lay south of Houston street in an area that until recently had been a refuge of impecunious artists. On their heels had come a trickle of residents, like Mollie, who were able to appreciate the unique qualities of the old buildings without expecting great amenities.

That, too, had changed as "gentrification" set in. Where there had once been family delicatessens and blue-collar bars there were now art galleries, trendy restaurants, exclusive boutiques. Mollie took it all in stride, viewing the changing street scene with innocent enjoyment.

It was that quality of innocence that most struck Sebastian. She was utterly unfeigned in her pleasure, uninhibited in her response. Not unlike a child, yet with all the beauty and maturity of a woman.

Deep within him a cold, hard kernel of cynicism was melting. It had formed over the long years in response to all he had seen and done, almost as a callus over his soul. The thought of opening himself to thoughts and feelings he had not allowed in years was frightening.

Yet when he looked at Mollie, listened to her laughter, felt the warmth of her smile, he couldn't help but think that the fear was worth confronting, and conquering.

At lunchtime, they found seats at a sidewalk café and settled back to enjoy the passing parade. But first Sebastian had to excuse himself a moment. "I've got to make a call," he told her. "I'll be right back."

He made his way to the back of the small, crowded restaurant, where there was a pay phone. Another patron had just come out of the nearby men's room, and he waited until he was gone before placing his call.

The phone was answered on the first ring. "Columbus Plumbing Supply. May I help you?"

"This is Eagle. I need a status report."

"One moment please."

He held on, knowing that his words had been automatically recorded and were being compared with his voice print identification. When that was done, he was put through to the appropriate party.

"Messenger here. Where are you?"

Eagle told him, using the standard system of coordinates known only to those within the organization. On the off chance that the call was tapped, his location would not be revealed. He would have hung up before the call could be traced.

"We have a report from cleanup," Messenger said. "Identification is consistent with earlier communications."

So the two men he had shot in the tunnel had been traced to the terrorist group. He was hardly surprised, even though he wished it could have been different.

"There's also been another letter," his control went on. "We have a deadline of seventy-two hours."

"Still no proof that they definitely have it?"

"Afraid not. But there is an added problem." He paused for a moment, then said, "The girl."

"Forget her, she isn't involved."

"Of course she is. How much does she know?"

"Nothing," Sebastian insisted.

"Still, she's a loose end and you know how we feel about those. I take it she's with you?"

When Sebastian admitted she was, Messenger said, "Fine, keep her there. I'll arrange immediate pickup and have her taken to one of the safe houses."

"No." His instant rejection of that perfectly reasonable course demanded some explanation. "She wouldn't agree."

Messenger's silence was eloquent. What difference did it make whether Mollie agreed? The organization was expert at getting people to cooperate whether they wanted to or not.

Which was precisely why Sebastian did not want Mollie to fall into their hands. "I'll look after her myself."

"And complete the mission? That's taking on a bit much, don't you think?"

"Nonetheless, that's how it's going to be." Inwardly he thanked the harsh realities of the situation that let him make such a demand. The organization had no time to get another man in place, but even if they had, he wouldn't have been on Sebastian's level. There were some advantages to seniority after all.

Not that he had any illusions about how long he would be allowed to have his own way. Unless definite progress was made, and soon, the organization would intervene.

But in the meantime, he would do everything possible both to bring the mission to a successful conclusion and keep Mollie safe.

"Have someone go by her apartment and pick up some clothes for her. Oh, and don't forget her cat."

"Cat?" Messenger said. He was a dog-man himself.

"That's right. I'll be in touch again after we've gone to ground."

His control would have to be satisfied with that. Sebastian had never made any secret of the fact that if he ever needed to go into hiding, he wouldn't use a safe house. Not that he really thought there were security leaks within the organization, he just didn't see any point in taking the chance. Too many other agents on all sides had died because they depended on others for their security; that was a mistake he would not make.

When he returned to the table, Mollie was sipping a glass of white wine and staring out at the street. A cold bottle of his favorite beer was open and waiting.

"How did you guess?" he asked after he had taken a long swallow. The day was becoming hot, hardly unusual for the first week of July.

"There was beer in your refrigerator. I noticed it when I made myself a cup of tea last night."

"And here I thought you were psychic."

His attempt at lightness didn't fool Mollie. Quietly, she asked, "Is everything all right?"

Reluctantly, he shook his head. "There is a problem." In as few words as possible, he told her what he had just learned and why he felt it necessary for both of them to disappear temporarily. When he finished she was pale, but her eyes on his were steady.

"Where are we going?"

"Connecticut. I have a house there that no one knows about."

"What about Mehitabel?"

"She'll be picked up."

"You mean they can just get inside my apartment...." She had the true New Yorker's horror of such things.

"Your security is pretty good, but they're experts. Don't worry," he added. "Nothing will be damaged."

She wasn't worried about that; rather, she was thinking of how tenuous privacy was when it could be violated so easily.

Sebastian watched the play of emotions over her face and sighed inwardly. This was going to be very hard on her, and there was only a limited amount he could do to make it easier. Softly, he said, "I'm sorry, Mollie."

She shrugged and reached for her wine. "There's nothing for you to be sorry about. It was my choice to get involved."

He wondered if she regretted it, but couldn't bring himself to ask.

Chapter 8

In addition to his own safe house, Sebastian also had a second car kept in a garage well away from his apartment. He and Mollie spent an hour or so on various subways losing whoever might be following them. When he was absolutely sure they had succeeded, they collected the car and were soon on their way out of New York.

They made one stop, in upper Manhattan, underneath the elevated tracks of the commuter train that ran from the city to the suburbs. Mollie remained in the car while Sebastian got out and walked over to a black sedan parked nearby. She couldn't hear what was being said, but she did make out the deep scratch running down the face of the man who handed over a suitcase and a cat carrier.

Sebastian was grinning when he returned and handed her Mehitabel. "He swears she's part leopard. Gave him a hell of a time."

"Just doing her job as a watch cat," Mollie murmured as she freed a very offended Mehitabel from the carrier. "Were there any other problems?"

He assured her there hadn't been, and that her apartment had been left secure.

Traffic was light all the way to Connecticut. Worn out from lack of sleep and too much tension, Mollie fell asleep. Mehitabel curled up on her lap, but kept a close eye on Sebastian.

They reached the house in late afternoon. It was far removed from the fashionable part of Connecticut, where houses stood on acre lots one after the other. This was farming country, though many of the farms had long since been abandoned.

Sebastian's house was reached by a back road that led in turn to a private lane, neither of which was paved. Surrounded by several hundred acres seeded with traps for unwanted visitors, it was as secure as any place could be.

Despite the various devices he had installed, the key ingredient in that security was his anonymity. No one in the quiet community knew him by his true name, or had any idea of where he normally lived and worked. Certainly no one was aware of his involvement with the organization.

So far as his few neighbors were concerned, he was a businessman named Howard Steel who occasion-

ally liked to get away from it all. He wasn't so stand-
offish as to draw unwanted attention to himself, but
neither did he go out of his way to be friendly. New
England reserve did the rest and assured that he would
be left alone.

Mollie was still asleep when he parked the car in
front of the ramshackle farmhouse. Sebastian carefully lifted Mehitabel from her lap.

"Behave yourself," he whispered to the cat as he
returned her to the carrier. She glared at him, but
otherwise didn't protest.

Gently, he eased Mollie into his arms. She nestled
against him as though she had always belonged there.
He stared at her for a moment before heading for the
house. The front door looked perfectly ordinary, but
in fact it was made of steel and could not be opened by
any key.

Standing on what looked like a door mat but was
actually an extremely sensitive pad, he waited while a
hidden camera scanned him , then relayed the result to
the computer that guarded the house. Only when it
was matched to the permanent record was he admitted.

When he stepped inside, the door swung shut automatically behind him. He carried Mollie up the
stairs, hesitating a moment on the landing. There was
a guest room, furnished but never used. He considered putting her in there, but only briefly. There was
no sense trying to fool himself, or her.

She did not wake when he slipped her shoes off and eased her under the cool cotton sheet. Moments later he was back with Mehitabel, who glanced around suspiciously before jumping onto the bed and curling up beside Mollie. "Keep an eye on her," Sebastian instructed before he went back downstairs to finish unloading the car.

They had stopped on the way to pick up groceries. He kept the house well-stocked except for fresh foods, so there wasn't all that much to put away. When he had finished, and put Mollie's suitcase in his room, he went down to the basement.

Only there could the true purpose of the house be seen. A large, freestanding metal cabinet housed the computer and communications equipment. With it, he could not only continually monitor and protect his surroundings, but he could also be in contact with anyone he chose within minutes.

The calls would be untraceable, since they were not made on public phone lines but rather used the completely separate network restricted to top secret government use. Sebastian's unique combination of skills and experience had enabled him to penetrate it.

A quick check of the computer confirmed that no one had attempted to enter the house during his absence. There had been one intrusion onto the land, near a pond he knew was a favorite swimming hole for local boys. It was close enough to his borders for him not to mind, particularly since he was certain they had gone no further.

His next step was to call Messenger. "About time," his control said testily. "I suppose you're still in the country somewhere?"

Sebastian couldn't blame him for being short-tempered; Messenger had been trying for years to discover the location of his safe house and took it as a personal affront that he had not succeeded. Even as they spoke, attempts were undoubtedly being made to trace the call. When they failed, Messenger would be in an even worse humor.

"I'm within reach of the target," was all Sebastian would tell him. "Anything new?"

"Woodman wants to know if that cat's had its rabies shots."

"I'm sure she has. By the way, there's no point trying to keep me talking."

"Don't be so certain. We can trace any call in the world, eventually."

"Not quite," Sebastian said quietly.

Messenger thought that over for a moment, then cursed softly as he realized the only possible source of calls closed to the organization: the secure network they themselves relied on. "Someday you'll go too far, Eagle. And I hope you won't be expecting me to rescue you."

"Wouldn't think of it," Sebastian said gravely. "Now, back to business, if you don't mind. Any further word from the terrorists?"

"No, but we think we may have a lead. It isn't much, but I've seen you work wonders with less." This last part was said grudgingly; Messenger was in no mood to be complimentary.

"Go ahead."

"We aren't absolutely certain, but seems that Abdul ben Hashir may be involved."

Sebastian whistled softly. He was slightly acquainted with the Libyan businessman, having run up against him once or twice before. "Doesn't he generally try to keep his hands clean?"

"Up until now. It looks as though this is the big one for him, and he's pulling out all the stops."

"I see." Sebastian thought for a moment, then said, "I may pay him a visit soon, but first I want to check the tunnel again."

"They're watching it."

"Of course, but there's another entrance I don't think they know about. I'll use that."

Messenger agreed, mainly because he had no choice; long experience had taught him that Eagle would follow his own course no matter what anyone else thought. Only an unparalleled record of success on the most difficult missions made that tolerable.

"Watch out for yourself," he said gruffly before they hung up. "I'd hate to have anything happen to you before I'm ready for it to happen."

Eagle chuckled. He and Messenger had worked together for many years; they understood each other, even if they didn't always agree. "Tell Alpha not to worry. The organization will come through, as always."

"I'll remind him of that when our budget is next up for review," Messenger said. "Provided we can indeed deliver."

They had better, considering what was at stake. Sebastian was still thinking about that when he went back upstairs. After checking on Mollie to make sure she was still asleep, he took a couple of steaks from the freezer, left them out to defrost, and settled down in the living room to read.

The book he chose was Walter Lord's *The Dawn's Early Light,* the hour-by-hour recreation of the climactic battle of the War of 1812, the burning of Washington. He was quickly caught up in the events of the summer of 1814, when the fate of the infant United States had hung in the balance.

So involved was he that he lost track of time, not noticing when the light began to fade outside. Only when Mehitabel appeared at the foot of the stairs and meowed at him did he put the book down.

"Is she awake?"

The cat twitched her tail and strolled into the kitchen, where he had thoughtfully put out a bowl of water and dish of food. Sebastian unfolded himself from the chair and stood up. His head still throbbed slightly, but other than that he felt fine, which was just as well considering what he had planned for later that night.

When he reached the bedroom, Mollie was sitting up, looking somewhat befuddled. He smiled gently. "You had quite a nap. I guess you needed it."

"I guess. What time is it?"

"Almost 8:00 P.M. Are you hungry?"

By way of an answer, her stomach growled. She smiled ruefully. "Starved."

"I'll start dinner. Come down whenever you're ready."

She followed him into the kitchen a few minutes later, after pausing in the bathroom long enough to freshen up. Her T-shirt and skirt were wrinkled, but she hadn't wanted to take the time to unpack, not when she was still so uncertain about what was going on.

On her way out the door, she had noticed a second bedroom across the hall. It was cozily furnished but lacked the lived-in air of the other.

"Is that your room I was sleeping in?" she asked after he had handed her a before-dinner glass of wine.

"It is."

"Don't you...uh...think you're presuming a lot?"

His gray eyes met hers evenly. "No, but there's always the guest room if you prefer it."

Which wasn't to say that she would. Oh, not that she thought he would bring any pressure to bear on her, but that might very well not be necessary. She was creating quite enough pressure for herself just thinking about what it would be like to be with him.

Sex for Mollie had always been a rather hypothetical subject; she had all the normal interest in it, but virtually no experience. Her friend, Lisa, had sworn that she must be the only twenty-six-year-old virgin left in New York, but Mollie wondered if that were true. She couldn't believe that she was the only woman who refused to settle for anything less than mutual respect and commitment.

Which brought up the question of why she was even considering going to bed with Sebastian. Of all the men she couldn't expect to have a future with, he surely was at the top of the list.

A secret agent, for heaven's sake, involved in Lord only knew what. The kind of man who went around with a gun under his arm, who could choke the life out of a person with almost no effort, who coped with death and danger as a routine part of the job.

What did they have in common except a love of history and books, and a certain fondness for cats, if the delicately shredded tuna he had placed in a bowl for Mehitabel was anything to go by?

"Sebastian," she said softly as she took a seat at the rough oak table, "I really think we need to talk."

He nodded solemnly. "Over dinner. It's almost ready."

He had prepared grilled steaks with herb butter, crisp french bread, and a salad of endive and tomato. Accompanied by an excellent cabernet sauvignon, it was as good a meal as could be found in any restaurant.

They ate in the kitchen, which had been left much as it was when the house served a working farm. Glass-fronted cabinets, scratched wooden counters and a porcelain sink were artifacts many a New York designer would have killed for.

"You realize," Mollie said with a smile, "that you're sitting on a gold mine. Those cabinets alone would bring a fortune on the East Side."

"Fellow who owns the next piece of land sold his barn recently for enough to build himself a new one *and* buy a tractor. He thought the architect who bought it was crazy, but the man had a right to be parted from his money."

"How did you find this place?" she asked, selecting a piece of warm bread from the basket he offered.

"I was rock climbing not far from here and noticed the For Sale sign. I'd been thinking that it would be nice to have a place to really get away from it all, and this seemed to fit the bill."

"Rock climbing? Somehow that seems to suit you."

He lifted an eyebrow quizzically. "How so?"

"Because it requires you to pit all of yourself against an obstacle," she said thoughtfully. "Your physical strength, intelligence, courage and so on. In that respect, it's like your work as an agent. But it's also different, because you're testing yourself against nature, which, however dangerous it may be, is free of the deliberate cruelty you must often see in other people."

"What do you do when you're not being a librarian?" Sebastian asked slowly. "Read tarot cards? Interpret tea leaves?"

His slightly caustic tone hurt her. She took it as an attempt to deny her access to his inner self. "I'm sorry if I've offended you," she said quietly, "but you really can't expect me to simply take you at face value, not if there's going to be anything more between us."

Sebastian was already embarrassed by his defensiveness. He was simply unused to having his deeper feelings and motivations understood by anyone, let alone by a woman he really had not known very long. But then, he shouldn't be surprised by her perceptiveness. He had sensed all along that she was someone very special.

"I'm the one who should be sorry," he said gently. "Please try to bear with me. After so many years of disguising myself, it's hard to drop the subterfuge."

Mollie nodded sympathetically, her wounded feelings soothed. "Would you mind telling me how you got involved in all this, and for that matter, what all this *is*?"

He hesitated. What she was asking went against the deepest grain. Only a handful of people knew the truth about him. To reveal it to her required a leap of faith he wasn't sure he could make. Yet the alternative was at least equally unpalatable.

He chewed a bite of his steak reflectively before he said, "My involvement started ten years ago. I was twenty-four, bumming around Europe after finishing up work on my doctorate. I'd planned to spend the summer there before returning to take up my teaching job."

Take 4 Books
–an Umbrella & Mystery Gift–
FREE

And preview exciting new Silhouette Intimate Moments
novels every month — as soon as they're published!

Silhouette Intimate Moments®

Yes...Get 4
Silhouette Intimate Moments
novels (a $10.00 value), a
Folding Umbrella & Mystery Gift FREE!

Catherine Coulter's AFTERSHOCKS.
When Dr. Elliot Mallory met
Georgina, everything between them
seemed so right. Yet, Georgina was
just beginning a promising career, and
a life with him would cheat her out of
so many things. Elliot was determined
to let her go, but Georgina had a way
of lingering in his heart.

**Diana Holdsworth's SHINING
MOMENT.** Derek Langley had been
smuggled out of Russia as a small
child. Now, with the help of an acting
troupe, and its lovely leading lady,
Kate, he had a chance to go back and
rescue his father. But when he fell in
love with Kate, he knew he might
never be able to tell her.

Nora Roberts' DUAL IMAGE. Actress
Ariel Kirkwood wanted desperately to
play the scheming wife in Booth De
Witt's brilliant script. As Ariel the
actress, she awoke the ghosts of
Booth's past. As Ariel the woman, she
awoke Booth's long-repressed
emotions... and tempted him to love
again.

**Barbara Faith's ISLANDS IN
TURQUOISE.** When Marisa Perret
saved Michael Novak's life during a
raging storm, it gave her a chance to
save her own life, too. Yet, she felt she
had to return to a husband who did
not love her. Which is worse? A love
with no future, or a future with no
love?

SLIP AWAY FOR AWHILE... Let Silhouette Intimate Moments draw you
into a world that promises you romantic fantasy... dynamic,
contemporary characters... involving stories... intense sensuality... and
stirring passion. It is a world of real passion and complete fulfillment.

EVERY BOOK AN ORIGINAL... Every Silhouette Intimate Moments novel
is a full-length story, never before in print, written for those who want a
more intense, passionate reading experience. Start with these 4 Silhouette
Intimate Moments novels—a $10.00 value—FREE with the attached
coupon. Along with your Folding Umbrella and Mystery Gift, they are a
present from us to you, with no obligation to buy anything now or ever.

NO OBLIGATION... Each month we'll send you 4 brand-new Silhouette
Intimate Moments novels. Your books will be sent to you as soon as they

are published, without obligation. If not enchanted, simply return them within 15 days and owe nothing. Or keep them and pay just $9.00 (a $10.00 value). And there's never any additional charge for shipping and handling.

SPECIAL EXTRAS FOR HOME SUBSCRIBERS ONLY... When you take advantage of this offer and become a home subscriber, we'll also send you the Silhouette Books Newsletter FREE with each book shipment. Every informative issue features news about upcoming titles, interviews with your favorite authors, even their favorite recipes.

So send in the postage-paid card today, and take your fantasies further than they've ever been. The trip will do you good!

CLIP AND MAIL THIS POSTPAID CARD TODAY!

NO POSTAGE
NECESSARY
IF MAILED
IN THE
UNITED STATES

BUSINESS REPLY MAIL
FIRST CLASS PERMIT NO. 194 CLIFTON, N.J.

Postage will be paid by addressee

Silhouette Books
120 Brighton Road
P.O. Box 5084
Clifton, NJ 07015-9956

Take your fantasies further than they've ever been. Get 4 Silhouette Intimate Moments novels (a $10.00 value) plus a Folding Umbrella & Mystery Gift FREE!

Then preview future novels for 15 days—
FREE and without obligation. Details inside.

Your happy endings begin right here.

"What happened?"

He smiled faintly. "Late one night in Paris I came to the aid of a lady in distress. To put it less poetically, she was being dragged into a car by a couple of apes. I'd been studying karate for a few years by then and was able to convince them that they really didn't want to bother her. Afterward, she and I went off to have a drink. One thing led to another, and she asked me what I was planning to do with my life."

He could still remember Madeleine's scornful reaction when he had told her. "Why not shape history," she had asked, "rather than simply teach it?"

"The upshot of it was that she introduced me to some people who made me an offer I couldn't refuse, although I have to admit I tried at first."

"You did?" she asked, hanging on his words. They were clues to a world she had never experienced except in spy novels. His life might be the stuff of fiction, but it was all too real. "What happened?"

He smiled at her breathlessness. "Nothing dramatic. I simply told them that it all sounded very interesting but also very dangerous, and I got all the kicks I needed climbing rock faces. They were very understanding, but six months later the offer was repeated."

"And then you accepted it?"

He nodded. "I'd had time to think it over, and in the process I realized something: I'd always taken for granted the kind of life we have in this country, but I'd never done anything to help preserve it. Plenty of men

of my generation fought in Vietnam; whatever you
think about the war, they did what they believed was
right. I was eligible for the draft but was never called.
Maybe it sounds corny, but it started to bother me that
I was strictly a taker, not giving anything in return.''

It didn't sound corny, at least not to Mollie. She had
been a teenager when Vietnam ended, and remembered the tremendous sense of disillusionment and
self-recrimination that had plagued the country. But
she had never been one of those who blamed the men
who had actually done the fighting. To her they were
simply decent people who had lived up to their re-
sponsibilities as they saw them.

"So you agreed to...do what?" she asked. "I'm still
not clear on who you work for or what you do."

"Besides running around in tunnels frightening
beautiful women?"

"I'm not beautiful," she said automatically.

He looked at her in disbelief. "Are you crazy? Or
don't you own any mirrors?"

"I know what I look like. I just don't see why it
should make such a difference."

His expression softened as he caught her faint wist-
fulness. "How has it made a difference, Mollie? In the
way people treat you?"

She nodded. "More even than that. In what they
expect of me. If you're considered beautiful, people
also presume you're dumb. And the men..." She
broke off, suddenly self-conscious about how much
she was revealing.

"The men," he coaxed gently. "What do they presume?"

Her eyes met his, challenging in their directness. "What do you think?"

"That you're fair game; that you'll fall into bed with them, and you'll be the greatest lay they've ever had."

Though his frank words made her flush, she didn't deny them. "That's about the size of it. And frankly, that approach gets very boring very fast."

"I can imagine." He could, especially given her intelligence and sensitivity. She must have decided long ago that most men were idiots. "But we're not all irredeemable," he pointed out quietly. "A few of us are even nice guys."

"Does that include men like yourself?"

"Maybe nice isn't the right word."

That wasn't what Mollie wanted to hear. Nice men rated very highly with her, men like her father and brother, and like the husbands of a few of her friends. Men who were strong enough to be gentle, who behaved with decency and honor, and who welcomed responsibility instead of shirking it.

Men like Sebastian. She couldn't believe that he was anything less, despite his disclaimer. But he had lived in the shadow world of fear and deceit for so long that he might be hesitant about emerging into the light.

He saw the faith in her eyes and was taken aback by it. To be given trust so freely, with such tremulous hopefulness, was beyond his experience. She made him think that all things might truly be possible, that he might be able to turn the clock back and become again the simpler, more optimistic man he had once been.

But that was impossible; nothing could erase the scars left on his spirit by a harsh world, in which only the most ruthless survived. He was part of that world, to the extent that he had almost forgotten any other way of life.

Almost but not quite. Looking at Mollie across the table, seeing the light dance in her emerald eyes and the soft ripeness of her mouth, he felt a thirst no sweet water or fine wine could ever assuage.

He wanted her with a savage determination unequalled by anything except the most basic desire to survive. Even as the small voice of conscience warned that he had no right to involve so lovely a woman in his harsh world, he knew that he could not give her up.

He would reach out to her as a man in a desert will grasp at a cup of water. As in a life-giving stream, he would immerse himself in her and hope that his thirst would be swiftly quenched.

Chapter 9

They had finished dinner and were sitting on the porch in an ancient swing that creaked rhythmically as it swayed. Through the spreading branches of the oak trees, Mollie could see the pale moon, riding swollen and luminous in a cloudless sky.

Beyond the grove of trees, visible between their sturdy trunks, she could glimpse a river turned silver by the moonlight. Silver edged the corners of leaves rustling dryly in the night wind, gilded each separate blade of grass, blanched the peeling porch railing where her feet, and his, rested.

"This reminds me of when I was a little girl," she said softly. Her head rested on his shoulder, and his arm was around her. She felt utterly secure and at peace. "We used to sit on the porch in the evenings;

Mom and Dad would talk, and eventually we kids would fall asleep. I can vaguely remember being carried inside and put to bed."

"How old were you then?" he asked, his thumb gently stroking her palm.

"Five . . . six. Willie must have been about seven. He's my brother," she explained. His touch made her tremble inwardly, but she managed to keep her voice steady.

"Great, an older brother and a father. Anyone else I need to know about?"

She laughed softly. "Just Mom. She has a mean right arm. Comes from years of whipping up biscuits and cakes."

"I take it you didn't grow up in a city?" He knew perfectly well where she had grown up, but he wanted to hear her tell about it. Partly because it would seem odd if he didn't ask, but also because he was enjoying the sound of her low, melodic voice wafting over him as gently as the scented breeze.

"We lived on a farm in New Hampshire. Mom and Dad are still there. I'm not sure what will happen when they decide to retire."

"Your brother isn't interested in farming?"

"On the contrary, Will would love to take the place over. The problem is there's not much of a living in it these days. He's married, with three children to support, so he has to be practical."

"What about you? Have you ever thought of doing it?"

She shook her head. "I love living in the country," she admitted. "But I also like the city. And I don't think I'm cut out to be a full-time farmer."

"When I was a kid," Sebastian said, reminiscing, "my brother and I used to vacation on a farm in Nova Scotia. I can still remember the special smells of early morning: bacon frying, eggs warm from the hay, milk so fresh it still had froth on it."

"Is that where you come from?" she asked.

"No, Dad was in the Foreign Service, so we lived all over. I was born in Bogotá; from there we moved to Toronto, which was how I came to summer in Nova Scotia. Dad got reassigned on a regular basis—Tel Aviv, Johannesburg, Paris, we made the usual rounds."

"It hardly sounds usual to me," Mollie said. "On the contrary, it sounds very glamourous." And it explained something about him that she hadn't previously understood: the aura of sophistication and self-sufficiency that hung about him, making it clear that he was a man who felt equally at home anywhere on earth. Or perhaps nowhere.

"I suppose it must seem that way," he said. "And there were good points to it. But mainly what I remember is the constant sense of being uprooted, of not wanting to make friends or really let myself feel settled, because before very long we'd be moving on again."

"Did your brother feel the same way?"

Sebastian nodded. "It was even harder on Derek in some ways. He's younger than me, plus he was born with a heart defect that slowed him down for a while. That's been corrected, but he always seemed to need more security than the rest of us."

"I can understand that."

"So can I, which is why I was glad for him when he met his wife, Mary Elizabeth." Sebastian smiled as he thought of his feisty, red-haired sister-in-law. "She comes from a huge Irish-American family. I truly do not know how many brothers, sisters, first cousins and so on she has. All I know is that they made Derek feel welcome right from the first."

The warmth in his voice as he spoke of his brother's family emboldened Mollie. Quietly, she asked, "Have you ever wanted something similar for yourself?"

His arm stiffened slightly around her, the motion all but imperceptible except to her heightened senses. "Occasionally the idea of a settled life can seem very attractive. But that's all it's ever been with me, an idea."

"Nothing you've cared to act on?"

"I couldn't," he said honestly. "The way I live, the things I do, can you really see any woman wanting to share my life?"

Truthfully, Mollie couldn't. She had difficulty understanding how the wives of policemen and fire fighters survived the burden of constant worry.

With a man like Sebastian, the problem would be even greater. He confronted an enemy to whom the worst violence and brutality were routine, and he operated alone, without backup to assist him if anything went wrong.

"Don't you ever get tired of it all?" she asked softly.

He couldn't deny it, at least not to himself. Lately he had been feeling wearier than he would ever have thought possible, a tiredness of the soul no amount of rest could cure.

At the organization, they talked about "burnout," the fate awaiting any agent who managed to stay alive long enough to confront it. Sooner or later the constant tension, suspicion and secrecy got to a man. He found himself making mistakes. In a business where there was no margin for error, that often meant forced retirement of the most permanent kind.

Sebastian didn't want to believe that he might be headed in that direction, but the possibility was unavoidable. He was not, however, ready to speak of it to anyone.

"Everyone gets fed up from time to time with whatever it is they do," he said. "That's normal. Don't you ever wish you were something besides a librarian?"

"I hardly think you can draw any parallel between our respective careers," she said stiffly. She knew he was deliberately evading her question and was hurt by that.

Sebastian cursed softly under his breath. He was so accustomed to leading people astray that he hadn't thought to treat Mollie any differently. Yet she deserved far better from him.

"I'm sorry," he said gently, turning her face up to him. His hand stroked the underside of her chin lightly as he added, "You have to understand, I'm not used to being open with people. I simply can't afford to be."

"Why not? I'm not the enemy, Sebastian. You can trust me."

But could he trust himself? He was starved for the beauty and gentleness she offered. She was a balm on his spirit and a goad to his body. Never had he wanted a woman as he did her.

Her lips were slightly parted. He bent his head, drawn irresistibly to claim her mouth. His touch was gentle at first as he held himself in strict check, but when she sighed softly and melted against him, his restraint broke.

The arms that closed around her were like steel bands. Her breasts were crushed against the hard wall of his chest. He bent her backwards, laying her down on the cushioned swing, his muscled thigh nudging between her own.

Rather than being frightened by his strength, Mollie gloried in it. She reached out to him with all the instinctive power of her deeply feminine nature.

Far from being any threat to her, he was the promise of completion. She had waited for him a long time, and now, feeling him tremble in her arms, she knew a fierce sense of gladness.

That the circumstances between them were far from perfect did not matter. She had been safe and secure all her life; it was time to take a few risks.

"Mollie," Sebastian murmured deep in his throat, "tell me now if you don't want this."

She heard the strain in his voice and knew what it cost him to even contemplate stopping. Yet he would do it for her if she asked. Whatever last kernel of hesitation had been in her dissolved. She loved this man, whether she would ever feel free to tell him so or not. At least she could show him with her body.

"Don't stop," she whispered as she moved provocatively under him. "I don't ever want you to stop."

Her need and the honesty with which she admitted it sent a wave of tenderness flowing through Sebastian. His touch lightened as though he had suddenly become aware that he might bruise her with the intensity of his passion.

She was infinitely precious to him in a way that went far beyond simple desire. He wanted to hold and cherish her every bit as much as he wanted to possess her.

He had never thought of a woman in such terms before. His lovers had been cut from the same mold as himself, sophisticated, experienced women who saw a relationship in terms of sexual pleasure given and received. They weren't interested in anything else, as indeed he hadn't been until very recently.

With a shock he realized that what he wanted to share with Mollie couldn't even be described as sex. It

had only the most tenuous connection to the almost
athletic displays of skill he had engaged in in the past
year. Though the physical act would be the same, he
sensed that nothing else would be. With Mollie, he was
setting out toward what was, at least for him, un-
charted territory.

Was it for her, too? Ever since he had first met her,
he had been aware of a certain aura about her, a kind
of gentle optimism that might appear naive, but which
served her quite well.

She was not ignorant of the harsher aspects of life;
she had simply chosen to protect herself from them.
He had known only a few people like that, and they
had all shared the quality of being wise beyond their
years while retaining an almost childlike innocence.

His hands trembled slightly as they moved along her
rib cage, feeling the delicate lines of her that gave way
to the fullness of her breasts. Beneath the straining
urgency of his body, he was acutely aware of her slender hips, the soft apex of her thighs, the secret place
of her womanhood. She was the epitome of contra-
diction, soft yet strong, yielding yet resilient.

He smiled faintly, almost in self-mockery, as he
wondered where men had ever gotten the idea that
they were the superior sex.

"Sebastian . . . ?" Mollie's eyes, darkened to the fe-
cund richness of a forest glade, were gently questioning. Had she in some way disappointed him?

In the next instant, she knew that she had not, as his
hot, moist lips nuzzled the hollow of her collarbone.

Sweet bursts of fire radiated through her, putting the lie to her often-felt skepticism about the description of lovemaking she had read in romantic novels.

Heroes were always unbearably virile; heroines all but swooned. She had enjoyed the escapist entertainment without ever making the mistake of believing it had anything to do with real life. Or would it have been a mistake?

Certainly no heroine caught beneath a glossy cover had ever felt more than she did as Sebastian gently held her trapped between his body and the cushion of the swing, teasing her with light, almost playful kisses until she was near to screaming in frustration.

She needed...wanted...demanded...she wasn't even sure what. All she knew for certain was that if he didn't satisfy the writhing, burning craving he had roused in her, she would never forgive him.

Her hands tangled in his thick hair, pressing him closer to her. Her legs parted further, instinctively making room for him, then closing to cradle him in a chalice of feminine power.

His mouth moved down the curve of her breast, finding the taut nipple hidden only by the fragile lace of her bra and a thin cotton shirt. She was hard for him already even as in another part of her body she was infinitely soft.

"God, how I want you," he muttered hoarsely as his teeth raked her lightly. The scent of her—sun-warmed skin, crushed flowers, and pure woman—filled his breath. He closed his eyes for a moment, struggling for control. When he opened them again, they burned with hidden fires that would no longer be denied.

He stood in a single, easy motion, drawing her up with him. Mollie gasped softly as she was held high in his arms, cradled against his broad chest. The effortless strength and grace of him made her feel suddenly vulnerable. She was no more afraid of him than she had been when their lovemaking started, but she was abruptly conscious of an elemental difference between them.

Sebastian might easily be seen as a man ideally suited to his time: urbane, worldly, with the casual cynicism of a weary age. But that did not change the fact that he possessed a more elemental side to his nature, the side that was probably responsible for his survival.

He was a quintessential male, a hunter whose spiritual brothers down through history had claimed and held the women of their choice with unalloyed ruthlessness.

She, on the other hand, was a woman, a nurturer who instinctively distrusted the fierce male urge to possess for the violence it too often led to. Not that she believed for a moment that Sebastian would hurt her, only that there were deeply running currents within him that he might not be prepared to acknowledge, or even understand.

Their mating—she did not shrink from thinking of it in such basic terms—had to be a coming together of equals. If he had any thought, however hidden, of simply branding her as his own, he would soon discover that wasn't possible. Possession worked both ways.

She smiled faintly when he kicked open the porch door and strode through it, shouldering it closed. He took the steps in quick strides, his breathing as even as if he had been carrying nothing.

The bedroom where Mollie had napped earlier was filled with shadows. She could make out little except the king-size bed carved from rough-hewn pine so fresh that it still smelled of the forest from which it had come.

He paused beside it and laid her down slowly, as though savoring the moment. "I've wanted to see you like this from the beginning, here in the place that's always been a sanctuary to me."

Mollie's throat tightened as she gently brushed the tips of her fingers across his face, feeling the clean lines of bones, the slight roughness of a day's growth of whiskers, the ridge raised by the scar near his eye.

"How," she murmured, "did you get that?"

"It doesn't matter." He lowered himself onto the bed, his arms braced on either side of her. "Nothing matters except us and what we can share together."

Mollie's brows drew together. She couldn't think in terms of only the moment, without reference to past or future. That simply wasn't part of her nature. She was linked to the continuity of all things, not set adrift on a current leading nowhere.

Sebastian sensed her distress and felt a pang of conscience. He could offer her nothing beyond this single time and place.

How could he even suggest that there might be more, when his day-to-day existence was fraught with danger? That was the way of life he had chosen for what he still believed were excellent reasons, but just then he resented it bitterly.

"Mollie, I'm sorry..." he said slowly, the words dragged from him against the opposition of his overwhelming desire. Despite how much he wanted her, he couldn't bring himself to lie. "I can't offer you more."

She stared at him for what seemed like a long time, but was in reality only seconds. The arbitrary measurement of time had no meaning when two spirits were linked, two souls communicating. In him, she saw honesty and need, honor, and a yearning so great as to take her breath away.

For his part, he realized with sudden stark clarity that her outward beauty was no more than the physical representation of her inner self. He had never made the mistake of equating aesthetic or sexual appeal with true goodness, but now in Mollie's case he saw that the two were one. She was exactly what she appeared, a strong, lovely woman whose beauty would only deepen with the years.

How would she spend those years? The thought of her with another man was utterly intolerable. He shook his head slightly, amazed by the intensity of his own feelings. If he felt like that before he had even made love to her, how would he feel afterward?

The answer was clear to him, although he didn't want to think about it right then. All he could really concentrate on was the driving need of his body that increased by the moment as he gazed down at her.

She lay with her glorious auburn hair spread out over his pillows, her hands lying loosely near her head, her eyes wide and dark. Her petal-smooth cheeks were slightly flushed, and as he watched, the tip of her tongue eased out to moisten her lips.

"Mollie," he groaned as he rose suddenly and began to remove his clothes. Her gaze never wavered from him as he rapidly undid the buttons of his shirt, snapping several in the process, and almost tore it off. Her eyes widened further, and her color deepened as she stared at him.

Bared, his chest and shoulders were even broader and more heavily muscled than she had remembered. Dark whorls of hair began just below his collarbone and extended across the width of his chest before tapering in a thin line down his flat abdomen.

His skin was the color of dark honey and shone with the glow of good health. He must spend a fair amount of time in the sun, she thought absently, but then, he must also get a great deal of exercise. She didn't have to be a physical fitness expert to know that she was looking at a man in peak condition.

Yet he had neither the ponderous heaviness of a weight lifter nor the stringy leanness of a runner.

Rather his body appeared to be a finely honed instrument, designed to suit both the man he was and the life he lived.

Not for the first time, she noticed the inherent grace that characterized everything he did, even so simple an act as unfastening the buckle of his belt and pulling down the zipper of his slacks.

She blinked rapidly as he stepped out of them, but still did not look away. Fascinated by the evidence of his arousal straining the thin briefs he wore, she moistened her lips nervously.

"Sebastian . . . I . . ."

"It's all right," he said gently as he leaned a knee on the bed and bent over her. "Trust me, sweetheart. Let me take care of you."

Mollie wanted nothing else so much as she yearned to give herself up to his obviously expert care. But her earlier confidence was fading as she was confronted by the reality of what they were about to do. Soft flutters of apprehension made her hesitate.

He saw her concern and was deeply moved by it. Always before he had sought to give his partners pleasure simply as a fair exchange for the pleasure he received. But with Mollie everything was different.

He thought only of her satisfaction rather than his own, wanting to give her an experience so intense and so perfect that no other man could ever equal it.

Gently, his lean hands touched her. Murmuring soothing words, he eased away her clothes, caressing each inch of satiny smooth skin as it was revealed to him. She arched her back, a rumbling purr coming from deep in her throat.

Seated on the dresser, Mehitabel blinked at them and turned her attention to the thorough washing of her paws.

Chapter 10

Mollie lay in the crook of Sebastian's arm, her head on his shoulder and one hand toying lazily with the sweat-dampened curls on his chest. Her breathing was slowly returning to normal, her heart gradually regaining its natural rhythm. Yet nothing could diminish the overwhelming sense of wonder she experienced at what had happened between them.

The resonance of their lovemaking still vibrated within her. It had been a revelation to her. Never had she imagined that passion could be so tender yet so demanding, or that pleasure could be the pathway to an entirely new perception of both herself and him.

Sebastian had been an extraordinarily gentle lover, particularly when he realized the full extent of her inexperience.

"Mollie . . . love," he had murmured thickly at that moment. "Are you sure?"

Caught in the fire-storm of sensation he had unleashed within her, she had barely been able to reply. Her eyes, the pupils so dilated as to leave only a ring of glittering emerald green, had stared up into his. He had loomed over her, big and hard, his body and what it was doing to hers blocking out all else.

She had felt the tremors of passion raging through him, smelled the heady aroma of full male arousal, basked in the heat pouring off him. Close as they were, she ached to be even nearer, to eliminate completely all separation until they became truly one.

"Please," she had gasped, "now . . ."

He had hesitated only briefly then, long enough to protect her, before gently introducing himself into her. "Give me your hand," he had whispered urgently, and when she obeyed, placed it around himself.

"Take me when you're ready, Mollie."

Impatience had flared through her, the desire to know all of him instantly almost overwhelming her. But even in her dazed state she had realized the wisdom of what he was doing.

Forcing herself to go slowly, she had brought him deeper into herself until the final barrier was broached and they were truly united.

He took control again then, moving within her with slow, steady strokes that made her moan helplessly and toss her head back and forth across the pillows.

The remorseless tide of sensation sweeping through her had obliterated all thought and reason.

In the blinding instant that the climax overtook her, she became pure sensuality. Sebastian's hoarse cries of fulfillment had mingled with her own before he slumped against her, drained by the force of his passion.

Remembering that now, she smiled to herself. Great-great-Aunt Amelia would undoubtedly be pleased to know that Mollie had inherited more than simply her looks. When Sebastian had at last raised his head, he had stared at her dazedly.

"How," he had murmured in the moment before sleep claimed him, "could a virgin make me feel more than I ever have before?"

Mollie had her own answer to that, but she didn't want to let herself hope for too much yet. She had closed her eyes, listening to the beat of his heart under her ear, and slowly drifted into sleep.

When she awoke it was light. She stirred reluctantly, reaching out a hand to him, only to discover that the other side of the bed was empty. Sitting up abruptly, she stared at it.

The imprint of his head was still on the pillow, and the rumpled sheets testified to how they had spent the night, but otherwise there was no sign of him. Nor was Mehitabel in evidence.

Mollie stepped from the bed and, suddenly aware of her nudity, pulled the top sheet loose and wrapped it around herself, tucking the corner in under her arm. She opened the bedroom door and stepped through, calling his name softly.

"Sebastian..?"

When there was no answer, she went downstairs, following her nose and the scent of coffee to the kitchen. The pot had been left on warm. A note was propped up beside it.

Gone out. If not back by evening, call 15-6789. Under the circumstances, would prefer you not leave the house. Sebastian

That was it. No tender words of love, no intimate reference to the night they had spent. Nothing but a tersely worded message that told her essentially nothing.

Piqued, Mollie dropped the note and glared at Mehitabel, who had taken up residence on top of the refrigerator. Judging by the condition of her dish, Sebastian had fed her before leaving.

"I suppose you think he's just great," she said accusingly. The cat blinked, but otherwise did not respond.

"The idea of leaving me here like this, especially after..." She broke off, not wanting to think of what they had shared. Good, healthy anger was by far the wiser choice. "If he thinks I'm going to cool my heels while he's off doing Lord only knows what, he's crazy."

She marched out of the kitchen to the front door and went to open it. The instant her hand touched the knob, a quiet voice said, "All exits are secured. Please do not attempt to leave."

Mollie had nearly jumped out of her skin at the sound of the neutral, vaguely mechanical voice. She looked around anxiously, trying to spot whoever else was in the house, before she realized what she had been listening to.

"*A computer.* It must be. But where?"

Her eyes hit on the door to the basement. She tried it gingerly, but to her relief it opened. A soft exclamation of amazement escaped her when she reached the bottom of the stairs and saw the array of sophisticated equipment gathered there.

In her work at the library, she used computers often enough to be able to recognize most of the pieces of hardware, but not to have any idea of what they did.

The amber screen on the terminal was lit. She approached it warily, only to jump back when she caught sight of the message scrolling across it.

"I am Guardian, the prototype fifth generation electronic security and communications system. I am currently at code green, all access points sealed. To alter programming, enter identification code and today's password.

Since Mollie didn't know either, she could only stare at the blinking screen in frustration until she became aware of how cold her bare feet felt against the basement floor. Muttering her annoyance, she went back upstairs and returned to the kitchen to find the note Sebastian had left.

15-6789. What kind of phone number was that? No area code or even a proper exchange. There was a yellow wall phone near the kitchen door. Hesitantly, she picked it up. Instead of the usual dial tone, she heard a strange whirring and clicking noise. Hanging up quickly, she stared at the phone.

He had said to call the number if he wasn't back by evening. Maybe she shouldn't try it until then. A glance at the clock above the stove showed her that she had slept almost until noon; hardly surprising, all things considered. It wouldn't hurt her to wait a few hours before doing anything more.

Reconciled to the need for patience, she poured herself a mug of coffee and went back upstairs to shower and dress. That done, she felt at loose ends.

After tidying up the bed, despite the memories it evoked, she returned to the living room and examined the shelves of books she had noticed there earlier.

Sebastian was an eclectic reader. She found scholarly treatises on history jumbled in with best-selling novels, analyses of foreign affairs snuggled up to classic mysteries, computer manuals sharing space with books of poetry.

The librarian in her itched to impose some sort of order, but instead she settled for picking out a mystery she had always wanted to read and plopping herself down in a comfortably overstuffed chair.

Mehitabel joined her there, curling up in her lap as a rare show of special favor. Mollie scratched the feline's ears gently as she said, "So you think it's right for me to do what Sebastian wants? Shows what you know. If he's not back by six, I'm calling that number."

Six P.M. could certainly be regarded as the start of evening. If he'd wanted her to wait any longer than that, he should have said so.

Even waiting that long was almost more than she could stand. The book proved unabsorbing, though she suspected that was more her fault than the author's. She would read a few lines and stare absently off into space, wondering where Sebastian was and, more to the point, if he were all right.

To make matters worse, it rained. Normally she liked few things as much as curling up with a book and listening to the splattering of rain against the windows. But as it was, the weather only deepened her depression.

She lost count of the number of times she glanced at her watch, finally annoying Mehitabel so much that the cat left her lap and moved onto the nearby couch. The storm worsened; thunder rolled across the sky, and bolts of lightning illuminated the room in ghostly white bursts.

Mollie made another pot of coffee, thought better of drinking it, and found a bottle of cognac in a cabinet. She poured herself a healthy measure and sipped it slowly, finding that it did help her nerves at least a little.

She supposed that she also ought to eat something, but the mere thought of food made her stomach pitch. Instead she tried to distract herself with music. Sebastian's collection of tapes, records and compact discs was as large and varied as his library.

The stereo equipment, kept in an oak armoire, looked daunting at first. She wondered if it was a first cousin to the snotty computer downstairs, but quickly discovered that it wasn't really all that different from her own beaten-up turntable and speakers.

With Beethoven's "Appassionata" filling the room, she felt a little better. The storm continued to rage for an hour or more, then died away slowly. Ever softer rumblings in the western sky accompanied its departure.

As the rain eased, Mollie stood up and stretched. Her muscles were cramped from a combination of inactivity and tension. She rubbed the back of her neck, sneaking another glance at her watch in the process.

Five o'clock. She would wait another hour, then call the number Sebastian had left. What she would say then, she couldn't imagine. Presumably whoever answered would know where he was and would have some idea of how to help.

Provided, of course, that anyone could. As the hours had passed, she had become increasingly certain of where Sebastian had gone. Their abortive exploration of the tunnel had been his second attempt to find whatever he believed to be hidden there. She couldn't believe that he would give up without making at least one more try.

Visions of him down there alone, hurt, perhaps even dying, wrung a moan from her. Mehitabel raised her head, looking at her somberly. "I'm so afraid for him," Mollie murmured.

Her voice cracked, and she brushed a hand across her eyes. When it came away damp, she shook her head tiredly. "I hate having to stay here, being so completely useless while anything could be happening to him."

Yet she had to admit that Sebastian was far better equipped to take care of himself in a tight spot than just about any other man. At least part of the problem he had run into before might have stemmed from preoccupation with her safety. Freed to concentrate strictly on his mission, whatever that might be, there was no reason to think he wouldn't come through fine.

Except that she couldn't shake the niggling fear that something would go wrong. It was made even worse by her inability to do anything to help. For the first time she understood how women must have felt down through the ages when their men went off to war and they had to wait helplessly to learn their fate.

Unable to sit still any longer, she paced back and forth across the room, pausing often at the closed windows in the hope of catching sight of his car coming down the road.

Each time he failed to materialize, her anxiety increased until at last it became all but unbearable. She crumpled up on the couch with Mehitabel in her arms and sobbed softly.

The cat bore it stoically, even going so far as to allow her fur to be dampened without complaint. Mollie lost track of how long she cried, but she did know that her eyes were burning and her head throbbing before she stopped.

What good was she doing herself? After the initial release of tension, her tears accomplished nothing except to make her even more miserable.

"To heck with this," she muttered, setting Mehitabel down on a pillow and standing up resolutely. She would bathe her face, put on fresh makeup and see about something for dinner. Even if she choked on it, she was still going to try to eat.

When she came back down to the kitchen, she felt better and more determined than ever not to give way again to fear. For that reason, she decided not to call the number Sebastian had left even though it was after six. She would give him another hour, long enough to fix herself a hamburger from the ground meat she had found in the refrigerator and perhaps even to force it down.

On impulse, she fixed not one hamburger patty but four, then decided fresh french fries would be nice. They might be trouble to make, but at least they helped postpone the time of reckoning.

As she worked, she kept up a running conversation with Mehitabel, one-sided to be sure, but still better than silence. The potatoes were peeled and the slices were sitting in ice water while the oil heated when something other than the sound of her own voice intruded on her consciousness.

At first it was so faint that she thought her imagination must be playing tricks. The hands that had been about to lift the potato slices into the oil suddenly stilled. Holding her breath, she strained to hear.

A car was coming up the road. She could make out the rumble of the engine and the sound of tires on dirt. The potatoes were forgotten as she raced to the window and peered out.

Though the storm had passed, the day was still overcast and the light less than it would ordinarily have been at that hour. She had to squint to make out the shape of the sedan that had brought her and Sebastian to the house the night before.

Mollie stayed at the window until she could see clearly enough to confirm that he was back, and alone. Then she returned to the kitchen and methodically continued her preparations for dinner.

The sound of the front door opening made her stiffen, but she did not turn around. Even when he entered the kitchen, she kept her back to him.

"Hi," he said quietly. "Sorry I got back a little later than I'd expected."

Mollie shrugged. "Did you? I hadn't noticed."

At her coldness, he frowned. Mehitabel had jumped down from the counter and was sniffing at his legs. Only when she had satisfied herself as to where he had been did she rub up against him.

Sebastian bent and rubbed her head absently as he said, "You're upset."

Mollie finally deigned to turn around and look at him. "Me, upset? Whatever gave you that idea?"

Before he could reply, she returned to her cooking. "I hope you like hamburgers and french fries, because that's what's for dinner."

"You didn't have to bother," he said. "I would have fixed something."

"Since I couldn't be sure when you would be home, and I happened to get hungry, I didn't see any point in waiting."

Lord, she sounded like such a shrew. Yet she couldn't seem to help herself. The long wait and the worry had taken their toll on her normally equitable disposition.

Sebastian's hands were warm and firm on her shoulders as he took hold of her gently and turned her to him. "Mollie, I know today has been rough for you, but there really was no alternative."

"Why did you go off and leave me like that?" she demanded, her composure suddenly breaking. "How could you, knowing that I'd wake up alone and not know where you were? Didn't you care?"

"Of course I did, more than you know. But what good would it have done to wake you? You'd only have had longer to worry. As it is, I seem to have gotten back just in time.''

''I was going to call those people,'' she said, trying to blink away the sheen of fresh tears. She absolutely was not going to cry again. ''Except that it was such a strange number, and there wasn't even a regular dial tone, and I didn't know who they were or what they would do.''

''They couldn't have done much,'' he admitted, drawing her closer. The full realization of how much strain she had been under filled him with remorse, yet it also made him feel paradoxically glad. Surely she couldn't have become so upset if she didn't really care for him.

The possibility that she might not had plagued him from the moment he had woken up that morning. Never in his life had he felt so insecure about a woman. The fact that he had given her great pleasure made no difference at all. He worried that she might have gone to bed with him simply to satisfy her curiosity, or that she might regret what had happened, or any number of other possible problems.

All his considerable discipline had been needed to put her out of his mind long enough to complete what he had to do, and even then he had barely managed it. The moment he was able, he was back in the car, speeding to her.

''I'm sorry,'' he said again. ''The number I left was in case you needed help; they would have been able to manage that. I locked the house to keep you safe.

There was a chance, however remote, that we might have been followed. There's no sign that we were," he added hastily, "but it's better to be sure."

"I suppose." Her anger was wearing off, replaced by immense relief that he was whole and safe, and back with her. Hard on that came self-consciousness. The memories of the previous night, kept in careful abeyance while she worried over him, flooded back in full force.

"Mollie, you're not regretting what happened...?"

"No," she said quickly. "Last night was wonderful. But today..." Her eyes dropped, hiding the full intensity of her pain, but not before he had caught a glimpse of it. "Today was very bad."

His arms tightened around her. It had been so long since anyone had truly worried over him that he didn't quite know how to handle it. All he was sure of was that he couldn't keep subjecting her to such distress.

Mollie saw the raw pain that flickered across his finely drawn features and was instantly regretful. Now that she looked at him more closely, she could see how tired he was. Wherever he had been, whatever he'd been doing, it had taken a lot out of him. And all she'd been able to do was go on about how worried she'd been.

Generations of stalwart ancestresses came to her rescue. She actually managed to smile as she said, "Enough of this. You can tell me what happened while we eat. That is, if you're hungry."

"Starved," Sebastian admitted, returning her smile. He was a little surprised by her sudden change in mood, but was grateful for it.

When she insisted that he sit down and relax while she finished fixing dinner, he didn't argue. With his long legs stretched out in front of him and a cold bottle of beer in his hand, he felt a great deal better than he had in a very long time.

In fact, he couldn't remember the last time he had experienced such a sense of relaxation and contentment. Watching Mollie bustle around the kitchen had an odd sort of rightness about it. The reality of the situation—that he could just as easily provide his own meal—in no way detracted from the pleasure he got from observing her.

The innate gracefulness of her deceptively slender body—whose curves he had fit so perfectly in his hand—made even the most mundane activity special. She smiled slightly as she worked, and hummed softly under her breath.

When the meal was ready, he stood up and pulled her chair out for her. Her arm brushed against him as she sat down, and he felt again that satiny warmth of her skin. Thoughts of food threatened to disappear until he reined in his unruly libido and turned his attention to the meal she had prepared.

"This is delicious," he said after a bite of hamburger.

Mollie shook her head wryly. "It's hardly gourmet fare. Sometime I'll have to really cook you a dinner...." She broke off, abruptly aware of how she must sound. Like any other woman trying to wangle a promise from a man that he really intended for them to have a future together.

That wasn't like her. She had never been dependent on any man for her own sense of self-worth or happiness, and she didn't want to start now.

But before she could retract the statement, Sebastian said quietly, "I'd like that very much, Mollie. When this is all over, I could wish for nothing better than that we'd be able to spend a lot more time together and get to really know each other."

"Is that possible?" she asked softly.

Sebastian was tempted, for a moment, not to be honest with her. It would be so easy to promise her, and himself, anything.

Not that he believed she was gullible, and he certainly wasn't, but he sensed that they both wanted the same things and would not find it too difficult to at least pretend they could be achieved.

But later, when the inevitable disillusionment set in, what then? To walk away from her would easily be the most difficult thing he had ever done. Even now he wasn't sure he could manage it.

"I don't know," he admitted softly. "We come from very different worlds. I'm not sure they can be combined. All I really know for certain is that I feel compelled to try."

"So do I." Three simple words, yet containing a universe of meaning. Different they might be, separated by an infinity of perception and experience, yet they shared a common desire. They were a man and a woman who had found each other and did not want to be separated.

How many other couples had felt like that down through the ages? Mollie wondered. And more to the point, how many had managed to stay together?

She didn't want to think about those who had failed any more than she wanted to consider their own chances. It was enough that for the moment they were together, safe in the old farmhouse hidden away on a country back road, protected by a state-of-the-art computer.

She smiled suddenly and at his quizzical look said, "I was just thinking, Guardian isn't exactly my idea of Cupid, but he seems to do a pretty good job of it. After all, he did keep me here for you."

"Did you really want to leave?"

She nodded slowly. "I wanted to find you. It seemed to me that anything that might happen would be worse if I couldn't share it with you."

He cleared his throat with some difficulty. "You realize that isn't too sensible? Although I didn't run into any trouble today, I might have, and the last thing I would have wanted was for you to be caught up in it again."

"Speaking of trouble," she said, as a sudden thought occurred to her, "I didn't show up for work this morning. They won't be too pleased with me at the bank."

"Don't worry about it," he assured her. "The senior partner got a call this morning, explaining that you would be unavailable for a while. He agreed to . . . as we put it in the trade, extend every courtesy."

"What does that mean?"

"That he'll cover for you without asking any questions. Of course, when you do get back you may find yourself regarded in a slightly different light."

He smiled as he considered what that could mean. "I've heard of cases where people who assisted the organization, even inadvertently, received big promotions and raises simply because their bosses were no longer sure what they were dealing with and thought it better to err on the side of caution."

He didn't mention that something similar had almost happened to him. More than once, he had resisted his department chairman's attempts to move him up the faculty ladder faster than he deserved. He supposed he'd be in for another bout of that when he returned from this latest mysterious absence.

"I wouldn't mind a raise," Mollie said with a grin, "but I like being a librarian, so they can forget any idea of making me a big deal executive."

"I've always felt the same way. About executives, I mean. They seem to spend all their time in meetings that rarely, if ever, accomplish anything."

He thought of Messenger as he spoke, remembering that his control had once been one of the finest agents in the field. He had come in from the cold—as trade parlance put it—when he sensed he no longer had the keen edge needed for survival. If a similiar decision was approaching for Sebastian, he was very glad that he had a different alternative.

"I like teaching history," he said as he got up to get them both another beer. "But this is the first time I've had an assignment that had anything to do with it."

"Obviously there's a great deal more involved than I thought. The security precautions you take make that clear."

"Unfortunately, more is at stake than simply an interesting historical artifact, or even something worth a lot of money. Although the historical value is definitely there, and I suppose what I'm looking for would bring an enormous ransom."

"Ransom? For something that involves more than money. Now I really am intrigued."

Sebastian looked at her steadily. It had been on his mind almost from the beginning that he would have to tell her the whole truth. Initially he had rejected that, but the further they came, the more he realized that she had to know. More than that, she deserved to know.

"When I first heard the story," he said carefully, "I thought it was crazy. The people who were trying to convince me had to go to considerable lengths to do so."

"But they obviously succeeded."

He nodded. "The evidence proved overwhelmingly that what they were telling me was true. However, I can't show any of it to you."

"You don't have to," she said softly. "I'll believe you, Sebastian, if you'll only give me the chance."

Her faith touched him deeply, all the more so because of the years he had spent in a world where suspicion ruled. "It has to do with something that happened during the War of 1812," he said slowly. "You may remember learning in school about how the capitol was burned by the British."

"And Dolly Madison saved the painting of George Washington. Of course, everyone knows about that."

"But in fact a great deal was lost. The defense of the capitol was so inept as to be all but criminal by our own lights. Rivalries among the officer corps prevented any real effort being made until virtually the last minute. As it was, the president and cabinet only escaped through sheer luck."

"It's hard to believe such a thing could happen," Mollie said. "We've been a world power for so long that it's difficult to imagine how helpless we were back then."

"So helpless that we nearly lost what may very well be the single most vital part of our national heritage. Fortunately, it too was smuggled out of Washington by very brave men, several of whom died in the process."

"How sad. I hope their efforts paid off."

"They may," Sebastian said cautiously. "Provided we can finally recover what it is that they hid."

"You mean we haven't yet? All these years, more than a century and a half, something important to this country has remained hidden? How could that be?"

"It's not really difficult to understand. You see, none of the men involved ultimately survived the war. Those who weren't killed in the siege of Washington perished a short time later. Until very recently, the record they left of what they had done was also lost."

"But what they took must have been missed. Or was it simply presumed destroyed in the fire?"

"No, it was missed all right, almost instantly. And when its loss was discovered, desperate men did the only thing they could think of. They concocted a copy, a facsimile, if you will, to hide the loss."

Mollie listened, fascinated. She couldn't imagine what could be so important that people would go to such lengths. "You mean some important historical artifact or document that's come down to us is actually a fake?"

Sebastian nodded glumly. "That's it in a nutshell. Until very recently, the real one was hidden in the tunnel under Cabot Brothers Bank. That much we now know for sure. We also have a very good idea of who removed it from there, and why. Unfortunately, what we don't yet know is how to get it back."

"What is it?" Mollie demanded, out of patience. "You must tell me."

Instead of answering directly, he asked, "Have you ever been to the Library of Congress?"

"Of course. It's a required pilgrimage for people like me."

"Then you've seen the Declaration of Independence and the Constitution?"

"Certainly. They're very impressive, especially the security that surrounds them. I remember a schematic diagram showing how they're lowered into a vault deep underground every night and—" She stopped abruptly, staring at him. "You're not trying to tell me that . . ."

"I'm afraid so. What everyone thinks is the genuine Declaration of Independence, the copy our side kept while another was sent to old King George, is in fact a very clever fake concocted in 1815."

"That's impossible," Mollie said flatly. "No one could get away with a deception that big."

"Actually, it wasn't hard. The Declaration wasn't considered especially important until after the War of 1812. That was the event that, more even than the Revolution, made us aware of ourselves as a people. Our victory in that war, against such enormous odds, set the seal on our existence as a nation."

"But still," Mollie protested, "too many people must have known what had happened to keep it a secret."

"On the contrary. The Declaration wasn't exhibited to the general public until the second half of the nineteenth century. By that time, it was only natural for it to be accepted as real. Remember," he added, "the fake was made not all that many years after the original. It wasn't even necessary to forge all the signatures; some of the original signers helped out by signing the fake. They were among the very few who knew what had happened, and they all agreed that something so central to the nation's heritage couldn't be admitted to be lost."

"You really believe all that?" Mollie asked.

He nodded firmly. "I have to, after seeing the analysis that was recently done. In secret, of course. The copy is damn good, there's no denying that, but it was never intended to stand up to modern methods of inquiry. The spectroscopy alone proved that the paper and ink date from several decades after the Revolution, not right before it."

Mollie, who knew the reliability of such tests, was suitably impressed. "All right, so the document on exhibit at the Library of Congress isn't the real Declaration of Independence. It says the same things as the original, doesn't it?"

"Word for word. The men who copied it were scrupulous about accuracy."

"Then what difference does it make?"

He leaned back in his chair and sighed deeply. "You've just put your finger on it. Ordinarily, the fact that the real Declaration was lost would be a regrettable but otherwise merely interesting historical fact. In short, big deal."

"So why did you become involved?"

"Because it hasn't stayed lost." He looked at her for a long moment before he said very softly, "The real

Declaration of Independence is being held hostage by a group of terrorists who are determined to use it to bring the United States to its knees.''

Chapter 11

In the aftermath of this astounding revelation, Mollie could only stare at Sebastian speechlessly. Her first thought was that she must have heard him wrong. Only gradually, as she took in his utter seriousness, did she realized that he meant what he said.

"Terrorists?" she repeated. "Hostage? You mean they're trying to use the Declaration to blackmail us?"

"Exactly. They've offered to ransom the Declaration for three billion dollars' worth of weapons."

"And if we refuse?"

"They intend to take it to a country favorable to their views—Iran and Libya are the likely choices—and make a big production of desecrating and then destroying the Declaration." Sebastian sighed. "It'll be great theater for the TV cameras."

"Would we sit still for that?"

"I doubt it. My guess is that would be the proverbial straw that breaks the camel's back. We've shown remarkable forebearance so far, but our patience has been strained to the limit."

"So there would be more violence," she said softly, thinking of all the images she had seen over the years on the nightly news, scenes of people suffering and dying because of the callous ambitions of brutal men.

"The entire Middle East is ripe for eruption," Sebastian said. "If we retaliated in force, every half-baked lunatic in the region would try to exploit the situation. It's not impossible that the Russians wouldn't be able to resist the temptation to try to make a few gains of their own. I hate to think what could happen then."

As did Mollie. She understood only too well that the superpowers maintained an uneasy peace by choosing not to confront each other directly. Should that change, anything might happen.

"But what can we do?" she asked quietly. "Certainly no one's considering giving in to the terrorists' demands?"

"Of course not. The only solution is to get the Declaration back before it's smuggled out of the country."

"Which is where you come in," she said.

"I've been following the trail of the terrorists ever since they first made contact a week ago. The first thing that had to be done was to confirm that the

Declaration had been where they claimed, but no longer was."

"Are you sure of that now?"

He nodded. "Unfortunately. It was just our bad luck that the journal giving the Declaration's true location fell into the hands of an unscrupulous antique dealer. He chose to sell the information to the highest bidder instead of making it available to legitimate historians."

"What happened to him?" Mollie asked, though she wasn't sure she wanted to know.

"He met with an accident right after the transaction was completed." At her surprised look, he shrugged. "It's not unusual. Those people don't like to leave loose ends."

"You sound as though you think he got what he deserved."

"I suppose I do. Is death too high a price to pay for betraying your country?"

Mollie had no answer for that. She could understand what he was saying; on the other hand, she couldn't help but shy away from the thought of such violence, especially when she knew that he might be its next target.

"What are you going to do now that you know they really have the Declaration?"

That was the part he didn't want to tell her about, at least not until he absolutely had to. "I'm not sure," he hedged. "We'll have to wait and see if there's any further contact from the terrorists."

"Surely there will be."

He thought so, too. It was inconceivable that they would give up now. The moves in the game were well known to both sides. After the initial demand and refusal came the most delicate stage, that of negotiations, which could be genuine, or could be simply a smoke screen for more forceful action.

In public, every government claimed it would never negotiate with terrorists. In fact, such contacts went on all the time. The niceties were sometimes observed by using intermediaries. Cooperative neutrals such as the Swiss occasionally helped out; other times respected private citizens intervened, but one way or another the conduits of communication were kept open.

Messenger would be seeing to that. Sebastian couldn't wait much longer to check in with him. "Let me help you clear up," he said as he rose from the table. "Then I have to make a call."

"I'll do it," Mollie insisted. "You go ahead." She had a fair idea of whom he would be getting in touch with, and she preferred to stay busy while he did so.

"All right," Sebastian agreed. Seeing the concern in her eyes, he smiled reassuringly. "But I should warn you, a man could get used to this."

"Don't," she advised him with a return of good humor. "It's strictly special treatment."

He laughed at that and went rapidly down to the basement, eager to get the call over with. After identifying himself, he was put directly through to Messenger.

"About time you checked in," his control groused. "Where the hell have you been?"

Sebastian was unruffled by the other man's grouchiness. "Where do you think? I've finished checking the tunnel. The document is definitely not there."

Messenger muttered a short, explicit word and sighed deeply. "Then the bastards have it, and we've got to get it back."

"Have you requested a meeting?"

"Not yet. You know it would be extremely dangerous."

Sebastian hardly had to be told that. "It's also our only chance, so there's no point delaying. The longer we do, the more nervous they'll get, and the more likely it will be that they'll pull something unfortunate."

"I'm aware of that," Messenger snapped. "Oh, hell, I'm sorry. There's no reason to take out my bad temper on you."

"Rough day?" Sebastian asked sympathetically.

"You don't know the half of it. Alpha is up in arms."

The President again. He was known to be something of a history buff, but other than that, Sebastian couldn't see why he was choosing to involve himself. "What's his problem?"

"He's at the end of his patience, that's what. Between the hijackings, the bombings, the kidnappings and all the rest of it, I sense he's ready to do something rather extreme."

"That," Sebastian said succinctly, "would be unfortunate." One of the things he admired about the President was his relative restraint in dealing with problems that were not susceptible to direct means of retaliation. The few times the United States had forgotten that, large numbers of good men had died in vain. He could only hope such a lapse in judgment was not about to occur again.

"If he's going to be stopped from doing something foolhardy," Messenger said, referring to the President, "we are going to have to settle this matter quickly."

"Exactly why I want a meeting."

"You're not thinking of—"

"Actually, I have no firm plans at the moment. I intend to play it as it lays."

Messenger groaned, and Sebastian could hear a paper wrapper being undone. "My stomach," his control muttered. "I swear it's gone over to the other side." He popped the tablet in his mouth and added, "You've always had a tendency to wing it. Remember Berlin?"

That was where Sebastian had gotten the scar near his eye. "What about El Salvador?" he countered. "Or Athens or—"

"Never mind; I get the point. Far be it from me to tell you your business."

"You've never hesitated before. What about the meeting?"

"I'll do what I can," Messenger said. "It will take time."

"That is something we have very little of."

"I know...I know.... Call me back this time tomorrow. I should have word for you by then."

Sebastian had to be satisfied, not that, on reflection, he really minded having to spend another day at the house. Or, more correctly, another night.

Mollie had finished tidying the kitchen when he returned upstairs. She looked at him cautiously as she asked, "Any problems?"

"No more than the usual. At any rate, we won't be doing anything before tomorrow at the earliest."

Her shoulders sagged slightly in relief. As reprieves went, it wasn't much, but she would take anything she could get.

"I suppose you're tired," she said, then flushed, thinking of how eager she must sound.

"No," he murmured, coming to her, "I'm not tired at all. You?"

She shook her head, not looking at him. As close as they were, she was vividly conscious of the breadth of his chest and the strength emanating from him. Yet it was also her memory of the gentleness he had shown the night before that made her breath come more urgently and sent heat flowing through her body.

The back of his hand stroked her cheek so tenderly that she gasped. Instinctively she swayed toward him, her palms flattening against his chest. "Sebastian...I..."

"What is it?" he murmured, his mouth nuzzling her throat. "Tell me, sweetheart."

"I feel so uncertain."

He straightened, looking at her. "About us?" When she nodded, he took a step back. "I wish I could tell you everything will work out, but I'm not sure of that."

"I know. You're being honest, and that's very important to me."

"But other things matter more?"

"Not more, the same. Security, a future, family, all the usual hopes a woman has."

"And a man. We're not really that different from you."

Mollie wanted to believe him, but didn't dare. She was resolved to live for the moment and not let herself count on a future that might never be.

"Let's forget what may or may nor happen," she said softly, "and enjoy what we have right now."

Sebastian did not need a great deal of encouragement. He was on fire for her. Any thought he might have had that one night with her would satisfy him was gone forever. Instinctively he understood that the more they shared, the more vital she would become to him.

"Mollie..." The palm of her hand was warm and smooth against his mouth. Turning her arm slightly, he pressed his lips to the flutter of life at her wrist, then moved upward to the crook of her elbow. She tasted of flowers and salt and some indefinable essence all her own. He remembered finding that taste all over her body, and his own hardened in response.

"Upstairs," he murmured thickly. "The bed . . ."

"I suppose we would be more comfortable." She smiled tenderly, surprised that she felt confident enough to tease him.

With their arms wrapped around each others' waists, they climbed the narrow stairs, playfully bumping and laughing with the ease of children. At the top, Mollie broke loose from him and ran down the corridor to the bedroom. He followed her swiftly, but allowed her to stay several feet ahead of him until she got close to the bed. Then he brought her down with a gentle tackle that sent them both sprawling across the mattress.

"Unhand me, sir," she demanded, in between giggles.

"Never. I may not be much of a knight, but I sure know a fair maid when I find her."

"Not anymore," she said, her laughter suddenly breaking off as she was trapped by the intensity of his gaze. To her deep chagrin, she felt herself blushing.

"No," he murmured softly, "not a maid now." His gray eyes softened with tenderness. "But not exactly an experienced courtesan, either."

"My great-great-Aunt Amelia was," she blurted, arching against the gentle caress of his hands.

"Was what?"

"A courtesan." Regretting that she had ever brought it up, she added, "A long time ago."

"Amelia..." He went very still above her. "Not Amelia Fletcher?"

She nodded, amazed that he could have known the name until she remembered that he was a specialist in nineteenth-century history, of which her ancestress had certainly been a part.

"You're a direct descendent of Amelia Fletcher?" he asked, clearly delighted with the idea. "That certainly explains a lot."

"What do you mean?"

He chuckled deep in his throat, an intensely masculine sound that sent shivers through her. "Only that I did wonder how an inexperienced woman could have such an extraordinary affect on me. You seem to have come by it honestly."

"That's ridiculous. Sexual...talent, or whatever you want to call it, couldn't possibly be inherited."

"Are you sure?" he asked, still smiling. "Amelia Fletcher was evidently a very sensuous woman. Every one of her 'protectors' fell wildly in love with her and, as I recall, she seems to have been genuinely fond of them. Isn't it possible that she had some special gift that might run in the family."

"But she was...promiscuous," Mollie protested. "I can't imagine being like that."

"I know you can't," he said gently, running his hands down her waist and hips, stroking the slender curves of her thighs. "But Amelia lived in a different time, when women had far fewer opportunities to make their way in the world. I hope you don't condemn her for what she did."

"Of course not. In fact, I admire her for...*ooh*...managing as well as she did. What are you doing?"

"Undressing you," he said patiently. He had pushed her shirt up and now, as she watched, drew the lace cup of her bra down to bare her to him. "So beautiful," he murmured as he lowered his dark head and suckled her urgently.

The tidal pull deep in her womb made Mollie whimper softly. Her fingers tangled in his thick hair as she pressed closer to him, seeking to absorb him into her own body.

"Easy," he murmured, breaking off his delectable tormenting. "I want to take all the time in the world with you."

They didn't have that, and both knew it, but how pleasing the fantasy was. Mollie succumbed to it without another thought, letting him do whatever he wished, and by the same token allowing her own impulses to flow freely.

Soon they were both naked on the bed, their limbs entwined, mouths and tongues seeking, arousing. His husky moans mingled with her higher pitched cries of pleasure. When he entered her it was with such slow, deliberate care as to make her feel infinitely precious to him.

Her welcome was absolute. Molten silver fires burned in his eyes as he felt the powerful contractions of her womanhood, holding him a willing prisoner within her. Their sweat-slicked bodies melded together until each lost awareness of where one began and the other ended.

A soft, almost keening cry of recognition echoed through the still night air as together they found the pinnacle of unity and were pierced by it.

Afterward they lay on their sides, still joined, as sleep overcame them. In the last moments of consciousness, Mollie murmured, "Please be here when I wake up."

"I promise," he said gravely, knowing only that it was a vow he wanted to keep for the rest of his life.

The next day passed too quickly. True to his word, Sebastian was the first sight Mollie saw when she opened her eyes to the bright morning light. With his hair rumpled, his firm jaw roughened by whiskers, and the sleep not yet gone from his eyes, he looked utterly beautiful to her.

When she told him so, he threw back his head and laughed with the sheer joy of being her lover. He knew perfectly well what other people thought of him. Women often found him sexually desirable; men tended to find him intimidating. No one had tried very hard to penetrate his deliberately remote facade, not until Mollie came along and ripped it away.

With her he was vulnerable. That realization more than any other was burned into his soul. Part of him thought he should resent her for it, but he couldn't muster the smallest twinge of animosity. Instead he felt

very much as he imagined a drowning man must toward the rescuer who throws him a rope. She refused
to let him dwell in the shadows, drawing him instead
toward the light. How long he could stay there was
anyone's guess, but however long it might be, he intended to make the most of it.

"Last one out of the shower cooks breakfast," he
announced, standing up quickly and heading for the
bathroom. Before he could reach it, Mollie had
scrambled ahead of him and was turning the taps on.

She gave him an angelic smile over her shoulder.
"I'll save you some hot water."

He patted the curved cheeks of her bare bottom and
grinned. "How about we share?"

She pretended to consider that while the water
warmed. In the end, he made the decision for her,
lifting her effortlessly at the waist and depositing her
with care under the shower, where he promptly joined
her.

"It's awfully cramped in here," she pointed out,
rather unnecessarily, since they were pressed so closely
together that a soap bubble would have had trouble
coming between them.

"Friendly, wouldn't you say?"

"Hmmm, very." She was becoming more comfortable as the initial shock of being so close to him in
such circumstances wore off. There was a great deal to
be said for snuggling against a large, strong, affec-
tionate male under a gentle downrush of pleasantly
hot water. She felt delightfully daring, even rather

primitive, as though the rest of the world had vanished and there were only the two of them alone in a sylvan paradise.

"What's funny?" he asked when she laughed softly.

"My imagination. It's slipped into high gear. I was just picturing us standing under a waterfall on some fabulous tropical island."

"Sounds good to me. What were we doing?"

"Oh . . . this and that . . ." She moved languorously, her erect nipple nestling into the soft, wet hair of his chest.

"I'm very fond of this," he said huskily as she moved again, her lower body coming into even more intimate contact with his. "And I'm absolutely crazy about that."

They stayed in the shower long enough for Sebastian to demonstrate that something Mollie didn't believe was physically possible could indeed be managed, and quite enjoyably at that.

It seemed only sensible after that to go back to bed for a while. They rose again several hours later and finally noticed that the day was especially lovely, bright and clear without being too hot.

"How about a picnic?" Sebastian suggested. "And a swim?"

"Sounds great." They filled a hamper with sandwiches, stuck a bottle of white wine in a cooler, and set off. Rather than use the swimming hole near the edge of the property, the one that was so popular with the local kids, they took a pleasant fifteen-minute walk in

the opposite direction, ending at a bubbling spring
that fed a deep, still pool.

Lichen-covered rocks surrounded the sparkling blue
water. They spread a blanket on top of them, near
where a towering willow tree offered shade. Mollie lay
on her back, looking up at the sky through the willow's delicate leaves. "I could stay here forever," she
said softly.

Beside her, Sebastian nodded. "I know what you
mean. Every time I have to leave it becomes harder."
Not because he disliked either New York or his work
at the university, but because it meant returning to a
world where he increasingly felt he did not belong.

She looked at him from beneath her thick lashes,
drinking in the sight of his long, lean form. His chis-
eled features were so much more relaxed than she
usually saw them. There was an air of contentment
about him that made her throat tighten.

"Have you ever thought of giving it up?" she asked
softly.

"Occasionally, but I've always known that I'd have
a lot of trouble doing that."

"Why?"

"Because working for the organization has been
such an important part of my life. Teaching is, too,
but in a different way. I'm not sure that I could give up
one *or* the other without feeling a great sense of loss."

"I see...."

He rolled over, propping himself up on his elbow so
that he could look at her. "Do you? I'm not a fool,

Mollie. I know that if I try to hold on too long, my luck will run out. I don't intend to let that happen."

"What's your alternative, then?" she asked huskily. "If your work means so much to you, how can you give it up?"

His gray eyes met hers steadily. "By finding something else that means as much, if not more."

They stayed by the pool for several hours, swimming naked in the cool blue water, letting their bodies dry in the sun, satisfying their hunger for each other, and finally even getting around to eating the picnic lunch.

When the food and wine were gone and the sun was beginning to dip below the trees, they started back to the house hand-in-hand. They walked in silence, neither needing words to express what they were feeling.

Mollie knew that Sebastian had made her an implicit promise back at the pool, and that he would try his best to keep it. But she also realized that he would never walk out on a job before it was done. Until the danger posed by the terrorists was past, she could not afford to let herself hope.

For Sebastian, that afternoon had brought him a glimpse of a future he wanted with all his being. To lie with Mollie in the sun, to hear her gentle laughter and feel the passionate response of her woman's body, was more than he had ever thought to be granted.

He yearned to share many such days with her while the passage of seasons brought their natural fruit.

Unbidden, the thought of what it would be like to have a child with her made his chest tighten.

He had always loved life, but never had it been more precious to him, perhaps because never before had he had so much to lose. Yet he would not have been the man he was if he hadn't still been willing to sacrifice that life for what he believed in. He could not stand by and see his country led down the path to humiliation and bloodshed.

Somehow he had to find a way to do what had to be done without ending up dead in the process.

When they returned to the house and he saw the message Guardian had left on the screen, he thought he knew how it might be done.

Chapter 12

I won't be left behind again," Mollie said. They were in the bedroom, where Sebastian had gone to change his clothes for the trip back to the city. The argument—there was no sense trying to call it anything else—had started almost at once.

"As I have tried to explain," he said with strained patience, "it is much too dangerous for you to leave here. Why can't you be satisfied with that and stay put?"

"Because I'm not some child who needs protecting. I was very hurt when you left me here yesterday, and I don't intend to go through a repeat of that. Why can't you accept that I have a right to decide for myself where I go and what I do?"

"Because I know more about the situation than you," he shot back.

"I know the dangers," she insisted. "But I can't stay here like some princess in a tower waiting for her prince to return."

Despite himself, Sebastian smiled at her analogy. He paused in the midst of buttoning his shirt and looked at her closely. She stood with her hands on her hips, her head thrown back, glaring at him. Her glorious auburn hair fell in disarray to her shoulders; her green eyes shone brightly, and the delectable lips he knew so well were drawn stubbornly together.

Their lovemaking by the pool had left them both pleasantly relaxed and very much at ease with each other, until they saw Messenger's communiqué. Much as Sebastian regretted how suddenly everything had changed, he could not see any alternative.

"Abdul ben Hashir is a very dangerous man," Sebastian said as he resumed buttoning his shirt. "Despite his pretense of being simply an Arab businessman, he's suspected of involvement in at least half a dozen terrorist actions."

"Then why is he still walking around?"

"Because nothing's ever been proven against him. He makes a great case for himself as a supporter of Arab-American friendship. He belongs to all the right organizations, knows all the right people, makes all the right moves. Every once in a while, he pops up on television telling everyone how misunderstood Qaddafi is, how he's really just a great guy who wants everybody to be friends.''

''People buy that?''

He shrugged and tucked his shirt into his pants. ''Who knows? The important thing is that you can't suddenly arrest a man like that without absolutely hard evidence, which we don't have, at least not right now.''

Mollie had sat down on the edge of the bed as she listened to him. Her hands were folded in her lap, and she looked very serious. ''That's what you're going after, isn't it? Evidence to convict ben Hashir.''

''My first priority is to recover the Declaration. If I turn up evidence against him in the process, all to the good.''

''And if you don't?''

''I'll worry about that if and when it happens,'' he said quietly, seeing no reason to point out to her that ben Hashir was hardly likely to simply let him take the Declaration and walk away. Evidence, or its lack, might turn out to be moot.

''You could be walking into a trap,'' she said, her hands twisting in her lap.

He stopped in the midst of reaching for his jacket and went to her. Gently, his hands closed over hers, stilling them as he raised her to her feet. Holding her close, he stroked her back tenderly. She trembled in his arms, and he thought he heard her choke back a sob.

''Don't,'' he whispered thickly. ''Don't be so afraid for me. Everything will work out fine.''

Mollie knew he meant well, but she couldn't accept his reassurance. Not when she understood the danger facing him. Ben Hashir, and men like him, stopped at nothing to get what they wanted. They might see this as a perfect opportunity to rid themselves of a powerful opponent.

"Please," she whispered against his chest, "don't make me stay here. I can't bear to be so far away from you, by myself, not knowing what's happening. It will be horrible."

His lean hands paused in the midst of caressing her back. Much as he hated to admit it, she did have a point. Were their positions reversed, he would deeply resent being left behind.

"All right," he said slowly, "let's compromise. You'll come back to New York with me and stay at your apartment. People from the organization will stand guard and let you know as soon as it's all over."

That was better than she had hoped for, although she was surprised he had suggested it. "Somehow I got the impression that you didn't want me involved with the organization."

"I don't, but since this whole business is coming to a head, it won't hurt for them to keep an eye on you for a few hours. Okay?"

When she agreed, he let her go gently and went downstairs to call Messenger. His control was less than pleased.

"You wouldn't let us bring the girl in when we wanted to, but now you expect us to play baby-sitter."

"I expect you to keep her safe," Sebastian said. No one hearing him could have doubted his absolute determination on this point. Even Messenger, who could outmatch the best of them when it came to stubbornness, realized he would have to yield.

But that didn't mean he had to do it graciously. "Oh, all right, I suppose if you really trust us to watch your...whatever the term is these days, we should be properly flattered."

Sebastian laughed softly, not the laugh Mollie so loved to hear, but a sound that more than one man had learned to associate with trouble of the worst sort. "I trust you to want to keep me at peak efficiency, so the mission can be successfully concluded. Worrying about Mollie won't help that."

"You won't have anything to worry about," Messenger said grudgingly. "We'll keep her safe as a baby in its mother's lap."

Sebastian couldn't ask for better than that, but he did have one further request. "If anything goes wrong," he said quietly, "I'd like you to tell her."

Messenger was a silent for a moment. When he spoke again, the sarcasm was gone. "I'll do that, and anything else I can. But I'm sure that won't be necessary."

"Of course not," Sebastian agreed. "We'll have it wrapped up before dawn."

He told Mollie the same thing when he returned to the bedroom to find her changed and packed. As he took her suitcase and Mehitabel's carrier, he briefly related his conversation with Messenger.

"You'll be in good hands; our surveillance and protection teams are the best."

"I appreciate that," she murmured, still struggling to come to terms with what was happening. How had she, Mollie Fletcher, librarian, come to be in the middle of an international intrigue, in love with a secret agent, and in need of protection by his associates?

Great-great-Aunt Amelia would undoubtedly have been thrilled, but Mollie felt differently. She simply wanted it to be over.

The trip back to the city was made largely in silence. Traffic was light, since most people who were going anywhere for the July Fourth holiday were already there. In a few hours, crowds would begin to gather along the riverfront to watch the fireworks display, but at the moment the roads were almost empty.

Too soon, they were at her apartment house and Sebastian was helping her from the car. He glanced up and down the street, nodded in apparent satisfaction and followed her into the building.

"What were you looking at?" Mollie asked as they rode up in the creaky freight elevator. "I didn't see anything."

"That's the point. There are three teams of watchers out there, and at least one more around the back."

"Where?" she asked, shaking her head. "With the street so quiet and empty because of the holiday, where could they be hiding?"

"Did you notice the water department truck parked at the far end of the street?"

"Yes, I suppose there's some problem." She frowned as a sudden thought occurred to her. "I wonder if we have water."

"I think you'll find you do. The truck's one of ours." He grinned at her surprise as they stepped off the elevator and into her apartment. "So is the panel truck parked at the other end of the street. And an apartment's been rented across the way, giving them a direct view in here."

"How do you know that?" she asked in astonishment.

"They saw us come in and signalled. I'm glad to know they aren't taking any chances." Mollie had clearly been given the highest level of security, undoubtedly because Messenger knew he would be satisfied by nothing less.

As they entered the apartment, she gasped suddenly and started to back away, coming up against Sebastian's large, hard body. "Take it easy, honey," he said softly as he nodded at the two men who had been waiting in the living room. "Meet Harry and Phil. They'll be on duty here." A glance at her white face made him add, "I should have mentioned that you wouldn't be alone in the apartment."

"That's all right," she murmured, shaking her head in an effort to clear it. After a moment, she managed a weak smile for the two men. "How do you do?"

"Just fine, ma'am," the larger, by an inch or so, said. She couldn't help but notice that they were both very big men, with the same tensile strength she saw in Sebastian. The three of them seemed to understand each other without speaking. A look, a nod, were enough to communicate whatever was needed.

Touching her elbow lightly, Sebastian said, "I'll see you settled, then be on my way."

In the bedroom, separated by a partition from the rest of the loft, he set her suitcase and Mehitabel's carrier down. The cat, freed from her confinement, leaped on top of the dresser and began to wash.

Mollie looked at the feline with a faint smile. "I wish I could be that nonchalant." In fact it was all she could do not to burst into tears, which might be appropriate but would hardly be helpful.

Sensing her great disquiet, Sebastian took a step toward her. Mollie held up a hand, holding him off. "No," she said huskily, "don't. If you touch me now, I don't think I'll be able to stand it."

He stopped and looked at her, at a loss as to what to do. Everything in him cried out to take her in his arms, hold and comfort her, draw strength from her nearness. But he understood her fear and knew that to ignore it would do both of them a great disservice.

His arms dropped to his sides as he said, "I'll be back soon and we'll talk."

Mollie nodded, no longer able to trust her voice. They stared at each other in silence until Sebastian turned abruptly and walked out of the bedroom. She heard him exchange a few words with Harry and Phil before the front door opened and closed again. Then there was silence.

She stayed in the bedroom long enough to get some degree of control over herself. When she finally stopped shaking, she returned to the living room. The two men rose as she did so, but she gestured them back into their seats.

"You don't have to stand on ceremony around me," she assured them. "I appreciate your being here, and I'll do whatever I can to cooperate."

They exchanged a glance before the one she had learned was Harry said, "That's fine, ma'am, but there really isn't anything to do except sit tight and wait for developments." Seeing the sudden flash of fear that darkened her eyes, he added hastily, "Eagle's the best. He'll have this wrapped up before you know it."

"I hope so," Mollie murmured, swallowing tears. She really couldn't keep giving in to her fear like this. Determined to distract herself, she said, "I'm going to fix some coffee and sandwiches. Care to join me?"

They allowed that that would be nice, though whether from genuine hunger or simply a desire to help her keep busy she didn't know. At any rate, she had the excuse she needed to fix a plateful of thick roast beef and ham sandwiches, slice up the apple cake she had made a few days before, and prepare a large pot of coffee.

As she carried the heavily laden tray back to the living room, Phil jumped up to help her with it. "This looks great, ma'am," he said quite genuinely. "Thanks a lot."

"I'd feel better if you'd call me Mollie," she suggested as she took a seat near them and poured out three cups of coffee. Playing hostess to these big, hard men had an oddly calming effect on her. Very politely, as though they were discussing nothing more than the weather, she asked, "Have you known Sebastian long?"

Harry and Phil glanced at each other. Harry swallowed a bite of his sandwich and said, "About five years, ma'am...uh, Mollie."

"Do you do the same kind of work as he does?"

Again the quick exchange of looks. This time it was Phil's turn. "Not exactly. He's got a lot more experience than us, so he pulls the tougher jobs. Not," he added quickly, "that tougher necessarily means more dangerous. Sharp as he is, I almost feel sorry for anyone who goes up against Eagle."

"I don't," Mollie said with sudden fierceness. "I just want them to be stopped so that this will end."

"That's what we all want," Harry said quietly. He was a big, sandy-haired man in his mid-twenties. Despite his large size, there was a kind of gentleness about him that Mollie couldn't help but respond to. "It'll be all right," he added. "Like Phil said, Eagle's the best."

Beside him, Phil nodded. He was a few years older than Harry, and perhaps because of that it was more difficult for him to give comfort. He had seen too often that being on the right side did not necessarily mean winning. But he had to believe that Eagle would succeed, not least for the sake of this lovely young woman with the haunted eyes.

Running a hand through dark hair already lightly sprinkled with gray, he said, "I saw Eagle in action a couple of years ago. He took out three Red Brigade members who thought they had him trapped. They never knew what hit them."

Harry chimed in with a similar story. Mollie realized they were both trying to reassure her, but talk of violence had the opposite effect. All she could think of was that Sebastian was going up against an enemy who would stop at nothing. And he was going alone.

She cleaned up the remnants of the meal after the men had finished, accepting their thanks and assuring them that she didn't need any help. Phil was on the radio to the other watchers, confirming that everyone was in place and there was no sign of any trouble. Harry was catching a quick nap on the couch; the men would sleep alternately so that at least one would always be fresh.

When the dishes were done, Mollie returned to the bedroom. Without removing her clothes, she lay down on the bed and tried to read. Outside, the summer twilight was giving way to darkness. She listened to the whir of the air conditioner keeping the humid heat at bay and wondered what Sebastian was doing.

She knew he had been scheduled for a briefing at the organization's headquarters before going on to a meeting with Abdul ben Hashir. So far as the Libyan was concerned, the purpose of the meeting was to discuss the U.S.'s capitulation to the terrorists' demands. But Mollie was certain that Sebastian had another purpose in mind. She tried hard not to think about that, and about where it might lead.

Mehitabel came over and curled up at her side. Mollie stroked her gently and was vaguely comforted by the cat's deep purr. She heard the radio crackle in the next room. There was a soft exchange of words been Phil and whoever was on the other end. When it had finished, she heard him wake Harry up, and the two of them talked for several minutes.

Unconsciously, she stiffened. Mehitabel raised her head and looked up unblinkingly. Mollie forced herself to take deep breaths, trying to relax even as she strained for any further sound from the living room.

When it came, she barely recognized it. There was a soft, apologetic cough; then Harry stuck his head around the partition. "Begging your pardon, ma'am...uh, Mollie, but we thought you'd want to know there's a visitor on the way over here."

"A visitor?"

"From the organization. He wants to talk to you."

She got to her feet slowly, taking in as she did Harry's strained look and the fact that he seemed to be saying a great deal less than he thought. "What's happened?" she asked quietly.

"I don't know, probably nothing. It's early yet."

"But you're surprised that this man, whoever he is, is coming here."

"Yes," Harry admitted reluctantly. He shrugged his broad shoulders. "Maybe he's just being polite. You know, a courtesy visit kind of thing."

Mollie hoped that might be the case, but she suspected it was not. After Harry had left, she went into the bathroom and took a quick look at herself. Her eyes were overly large, and she was unnaturally pale. Whoever this man was, it wouldn't do to meet him looking like a frightened waif.

Ten minutes later, when she left the bathroom, she had taken care of that. A judicious application of makeup put color in her cheeks and gave her the confidence to face whatever might be coming. Or so she thought until she entered the living room to find both men standing tensely near the windows.

"He's coming," Phil said. Harry spoke briefly into the radio, then added, "All's clear. Nothing's moving on the street except his car."

Mollie went to the adjacent window and peered out. She could see nothing except a perfectly ordinary looking sedan making its way down the block. It double-parked in front of her building, and a tall, thin man in a dark suit got out. He said something to the driver before disappearing through the front door.

"It's him, all right," Harry said.

Phil still insisted on confirming that when the man stepped off the elevator. Politely but firmly, he asked for identification. The man smiled slightly as he reached into the breast pocket of his jacket and withdrew his wallet, while Harry kept a smaller revolver trained on him. He handed it unopened to Phil, who flipped through it, found what he was looking for and handed it back.

"I hope you understand, sir," he said quietly, "that we can't take any chances."

"Of course not," the man said, his attention now on Mollie, who had stood silently throughout the exchange. "Eagle is not a man to disappoint, and I know he's counting on you to keep this lovely young lady safe."

Crossing the room, he offered her a thin, elegant hand. "My name is Messenger. I am Sebastian's control within the organization. I don't mind admitting that I have been very curious about you."

"No more than I've been about you," she said candidly. His handshake was cool and firm, as was his scrutiny. She returned both in kind. "Everything about Sebastian interests me, but especially those things that have to do with his safety."

"Ah, yes, safety." Messenger nodded. "That most elusive of human dreams. I'm sure you understand that we live in extremely unsafe times."

Mollie studied the aquiline features of the man facing her for a moment before she nodded. "That's been made very clear to me recently. Would you care to sit down?''

He accepted the suggestion and made himself comfortable on the couch. Phil and Harry had discreetly withdrawn to the kitchen, leaving Mollie alone with her visitor. She took a chair across from him and remained silent, waiting for him to explain his presence.

Long minutes dragged out before Messenger abruptly smiled. ''You're quite good, you know. Most people can't resist the temptation to chatter away and, in the process, spill all sorts of things. But you wait, silent, unmoving, for me to unburden myself. Tell me, have you ever considered entering the trade?''

''Trade?''

''The craft, the business, whatever one wants to call it. Spying is such an imprecise term. We do that, of course, but we also do quite a good deal more.''

''You're speaking of the organization? The one Sebastian belongs to?''

Messenger sat forward, his hands between his elegantly clad legs, and observed her carefully. ''It isn't like Eagle to be indiscreet. Quite the contrary. But all men have their limits. I have to wonder how much he has told you.''

''Is that why you're here, to find out what I know?''

''That and one or two other things. Do you mind if I smoke?''

When Mollie indicated that she did not, Messenger lit a thin cigar and sat back to enjoy it. ''Suppose you start at the beginning. Tell me how you met Eagle, what drew you together, how he took you into his confidence, that sort of thing."

"Why should I?"

The quietly uttered question brought Messenger up short. His cigar was momentarily forgotten as he said, "It's only friendly interest, I assure you. There's no harm in telling me."

"Except that what's happened between Sebastian and me is no one's business except ours."

"My dear girl, Sebastian and I work together. Not to put too fine a point on it, I'm his boss. You're perfectly safe in trusting me."

"I don't think so," Mollie said with a slight shake of her head. "Oh, not that I think you mean Sebastian any harm, but I believe your only interest is in seeing his mission succeed, and you'll do anything to bring that about."

"If you knew the purpose of the mission . . ." Messenger began somewhat testily.

"I know enough to understand that Sebastian is in very grave danger. What I can't figure out is why you've bothered to come here, to question me about things that are none of your business, when you should be concentrating on doing whatever you can to help him."

Despite herself, some of her anger and impatience came through clearly. Messenger regarded her with even greater interest. "Beauty, intelligence *and* spirit.

I'm beginning to understand Sebastian's predicament.''

At her questioning look, he elaborated. "Sebastian is a man who has always placed honor and duty above all else, yet suddenly he showed an equal desire to protect you. I was quite puzzled. In fact, I'll go further and admit that I was worried. It wasn't absolutely impossible that he had fallen into the clutches of, for want of a better term, a *femme fatale*."

"Me?" Mollie said in genuine amazement. Despite herself, she was beginning to like this aristocratic, almost old-fashioned man, with his dignified manners and quaint turns of phrase. But that didn't mean she was about to let down her guard.

"I hate to disappoint you," she said, "but I'm the furthest thing from what you imagined. There's nothing mysterious about my relationship with Sebastian. I love him, and I believe he's also come to care for me."

Messenger's deep set eyes softened somewhat as he listened to her. He wasn't a sentimental man, but even he could be touched by the reality of love. He could even pause very briefly to appreciate it before deciding how it could best be turned to his advantage.

"As you pointed out," he said, after taking another puff on his cigar, "Sebastian is in very great danger. As vital as his mission is, none of us wants to see him lose his life because of it."

Mollie swallowed with some difficulty. "No, of course not. I'm sorry about what I said, about your not concentrating on helping him. I'm sure you're doing everything you can."

Messenger nodded gravely. "Therein lies the problem. We are rather limited in what we can do."

"What do you mean?"

"Only that Abdul ben Hashir is the furthest thing from a fool. He hasn't stayed alive this long by taking chances with his security. Sebastian will not be allowed near him carrying any weapon."

"But ben Hashir will be armed?" Mollie said faintly. The image of Sebastian going into a den of terrorists without even a weapon to protect him was almost more than she could bear.

"Of course, "Messenger said. "As will be all his guards. Don't misunderstand me; Sebastian isn't completely helpless. Far from it. He's a master of unarmed combat. But the fact remains that he will be one against many. The odds do not look good."

"Then why are you letting him do this?" Mollie demanded.

"Because I knew he wouldn't accept the alternative." Regarding her steadily, Messenger said, "I'm hoping that you will. In fact, you might say that I'm pinning all my hopes on you. Both for the sake of the mission and for Sebastian's survival."

Chapter 13

Mollie took a step back and studied herself carefully in the full-length mirror. The woman who returned her gaze was a stranger. Dressed in a long form-fitting gown of emerald silk, her hair falling in carefully designed disarray around her shoulders and her face artfully made up, she looked as though she had just stepped from the pages of an elegant fashion magazine.

Messenger had wasted no time after winning her agreement. Barely had she told him that she would cooperate than he had summoned a hair dresser, a couturier and a makeup expert to the apartment. Within an hour, they had—as one of them put it—whipped her into shape, though he was gracious enough to admit that she'd given them good material to work with.

"You must look the part," Messenger had insisted when she asked whether all this was really necessary. "As the supposed daughter of a Texas oil man and his wife, certain things will be expected of you. Not the least of which is," he had smiled faintly, "a certain dramatic taste in fashion."

She had certainly achieved that, if the vision in the mirror was anything to go by. That she had also achieved a bit more was brought home to her the moment she left the bedroom and encountered the startled stares of Harry and Phil.

"Something wrong?" she had asked, surprised to see their professional detachment so abruptly dented.

"Uh, no..." Phil muttered. "You look fine, Mollie. Just fine."

"Fine," Harry repeated, a bit dazedly.

"Come now," Messenger interjected. "You can go further than that. You look absolutely lovely, my dear. Sebastian will be quite impressed." *After he gets through being furiously angry,* Messenger added silently.

"Do you think ben Hashir will be fooled?" she asked softly.

"I'm convinced he will be," Messenger assured her. "We have checked very carefully and are certain that your identity is not known to the terrorists. There's always a chance they might spot someone from the organization, which is why we aren't sending one of our own, but you should get by without difficulty.

"Which is why," he added, "you'll be carrying this." Handing her the snub-nosed pistol, he smiled gently. "Keep it in your handbag until you have an opportunity to give it to Sebastian."

"This party ben Hashir is hosting," Mollie said as she took the gun. It was cold and heavy in her hand, and she tried not to think about what it might mean. "How many people will be there?"

"About a hundred, which should provide you with plenty of camouflage. Mr. and Mrs. 'Tex' Bendel have been asked to allow you to join them as their daughter, but they haven't been told why."

"Yet they've agreed to go along?"

"Mr. Bendel does a great deal of business with the U.S. government. He knows better than to refuse."

Mollie nodded absently, her thoughts less on the couple in question than on the party itself. "Why is ben Hashir giving a party tonight? Most people are out of town."

"And many of them came back especially for this event, because, as it happens, ben Hashir's penthouse has a fabulous view of the river, and therefore of the fireworks display. That makes him very popular."

Mollie could understand that. The fireworks display put on each year by Macy's department store was an event looked forward to by all New Yorkers. Thousands gathered along the riverfront, while others watched from apartments and even from hotel rooms rented specifically for the purpose.

"It's rather ironic, don't you think," she said, "that ben Hashir is giving a party to celebrate the Fourth of July?"

"No one has ever accused him of not having a sense of humor," Messenger said dryly. "Now, my dear, let's go through the plan once more to make sure you've got everything down."

Half an hour later, Mollie was escorted from her apartment by Phil and Harry. Messenger followed. A separate car had been called for her. He saw her into it. As he shut the door, he said quietly, "Don't worry, Mollie. You'll come through for him; I'm sure."

She wished that she could be as confident, but as the car started up, taking her to her rendezvous with the Bendels, she was plagued with doubts. How would she ever be able to pull off so difficult a task? What if she slipped up, and ben Hashir's people spotted her?

Besides the normal concern she had for her own safety, she was desperately worried about Sebastian. In trying to help him, she might inadvertently place him in even worse danger.

But Messenger had been quite clear about the chances of his getting out without any sort of weapon. "Not good, I'm afraid," he had said when they discussed the matter. "If he were only there to negotiate, as ben Hashir believes, he might have a chance. But under the circumstances . . ."

He had let that trail off, seeing by the look on Mollie's face that she understood his meaning.

Seated in the back of the car, she tried to calm herself before meeting the Bendels. They would undoubtedly be curious, even apprehensive, and she wanted to do nothing that might make them behave unnaturally.

As it happened, she needn't have worried. Mr. Bendel, a big, bluff man in evening clothes and a Stetson, made it clear from the first moment of their meeting that there was no love lost between him and ben Hashir. Anything he could do to harm the Libyans would be his pleasure.

"I had no intention of attending ben Hashir's party," he said as they sat in the living room of the couple's hotel suite, getting acquainted. "Fact is, I thought he was damned presumptuous to invite me. But then an old buddy of mine from my Special Forces days called and asked for a favor. Well, hell, how many times does a washed-up old geezer like me get a chance to help his country?"

"Now, dear," Mrs. Bendel said softly, tilting her perfectly coiffed blond head toward her husband. "No one believes for a moment that you're either old or washed-up. It isn't fair of you to be fishing for compliments from this pretty young thing. Especially not when we've got to be going if we aren't going to miss all the fun."

"She doesn't mean the fireworks," Bendel said as he opened the door to the corridor and stood aside for the ladies. "Time was Honey could mix it up with the best of them."

"Still can," she informed him with a teasing smile. More seriously, she said to Mollie, "Don't worry, dear. We'll give you any help we possibly can."

"That's very kind of you, but remember, you're not supposed to endanger yourselves. You're doing quite enough simply by letting me come with you."

"Well, now, why wouldn't we?" Honey asked with a smile. "You're our daughter, aren't you?"

As Mollie learned on the ride to ben Hashir's apartment, the Bendels really did have a daughter, named Sue, who looked something like Mollie and was currently studying at the Sorbonne. "We're so proud of her," Tex said, "we could just about burst."

"She's coming home next month," Honey added. "There's a boy—well, he's a man now—she's known for years. I've got a feeling something's going to happen between them."

"That's just 'cause you've got a hankering for grandkids," Tex said. "'Course I got to admit, I couldn't ask for a better son-in-law than Chase. He's an oil man, too," he explained in an aside to Mollie. "Wildcatter, but one of the lucky ones. Made a bundle or two and looks to make more."

"His name is Chase?" she asked. "Maybe I'd better remember that. Is anyone at this party likely to know you very well?"

"Shouldn't think so," Tex said. "We don't get up to New York very often, and it's not as though we make a habit of mixing with the Libyans. But if anyone does spot us, they wouldn't recognize Sue. She's been out of the country for a couple of years now, and even before then she wasn't a big one for parties.''

"That's good," Mollie said, thinking how lucky they were that the Bendels had happened to be in town and invited to ben Hashir's party. Perhaps their luck would hold all the way through.

She kept that thought uppermost in her mind as they pulled up in front of the gracious Fifth Avenue apartment building and the chauffeur helped them from the car. Whatever else he might be, ben Hashir could not be faulted for his taste. His penthouse apartment was in a gracious, turn-of-the-century building overlooking Central Park. Parquet marble floors, stone pillars and a doorman outfitted in an elaborate uniform set the tone of exclusivity.

Mr. Bendel gave their names and they were ushered upstairs. Another couple had come in just as they did, so the elevator was fairly full. As they stepped off on the penthouse floor, the other man pointed toward the ceiling and said, "Abdul's not taking any chances, I see. Smile, we're all on candid camera."

Mollie's mouth was very stiff as she attempted to laugh along with the others. Entering the apartment, she was immediately engulfed in the noise and color of the party. Most of the hundred guests were already on hand, all elegantly garbed, the men in dinner jackets, the women in exquisite gowns. She was glad Messenger had insisted on outfitting her so luxuriously, since that at least gave her a chance of blending in with the crowd.

Two hard-faced men stood on either side of the narrow hallway that led into the large room where the party was taking place. They scrutinized each guest as he or she entered, seeming to miss nothing with their impenetrable black eyes.

As they passed the guards, Mollie took Tex Bendel's arm and smiled at him prettily. "I'm so glad you talked me into coming, Daddy. Why, I wouldn't have wanted to miss this for the world."

Her slight attempt at a Texas drawl, carefully underdone, made him grin as he responded in kind. "Sue, darlin', you just wait 'till you see how good these A-rabs are at throwing a party. Why, they could teach us down-home boys a thing or two."

I'll just bet, Mollie thought to herself, breathing a sigh of relief when they were past the guards. It was hard to imagine anyone with more on the ball than Tex Bendel, or his lovely wife, who had launched into a description of a party she had been to in Houston just the last week, and wasn't it such a shame Sue hadn't been back from Paris in time to go with her?

Chattering away, they made their way to the bar, where Tex got them each a drink. "I see our host doesn't follow the Moslem rule against alcohol," Mollie said after she had taken a sip of her white wine. It was perfectly chilled and of an excellent vintage. Ben Hashir was going all out to impress; judging by the looks on the faces of many of the guests, he was succeeding.

Everyone seemed to be having a very good time. A jazz quartet played in the background as waiters circulated with canapés. Through the floor-to-ceiling windows that took up one entire wall and wrapped around to the next, the New York skyline glinted like black velvet strewn with diamonds.

"It's so beautiful," Mollie murmured under her breath. "I can hardly believe anything bad could happen tonight."

"Don't think about it," Honey advised. She tilted her head toward a door that had just opened off to one side. "Come and meet our host."

Abdul ben Hashir had just emerged from what appeared to be a library. Before the door closed again behind him, Mollie caught a glimpse of book-lined walls and antique furniture. She was barely aware of them, though, as all her attention was riveted on the man shaking hands with Tex Bendel.

Ben Hashir was in his late forties, with thick black hair, black eyes and light brown skin. Impeccably dressed, he exuded a polished, cosmopolitan air that Mollie did not doubt was very effective. There was certainly nothing about him to even remotely suggest that he would be involved in illegal activities, let alone terrorism.

"Miss Bendel," he said smoothly, bending over her hand as they were introduced. "Such a pleasure. I had known, of course, that Honey and Tex had a beautiful daughter, but you surpass all expectation."

Mollie found his flattery rather overdone, but she accepted it charmingly. "How sweet of you to say so, Mr. ben Hashir. Might I say in return that I'm just fascinated to meet you? You're my very first Arab."

For an instant, she thought she might have laid it on too thickly, but the flicker of surprise died in ben Hashir's eyes, and he looked at her with cynical interest. "Then you must allow me to explain to you all about my people and our ways. I'm sure you will find them fascinating."

"I'll just bet you will," Tex muttered a few moments later as their host excused himself to see to other guests—briefly, he assured Mollie. "Are you sure it's such a good idea to egg him on like that?" Tex asked.

"I don't know what else to do," Mollie admitted. "Somehow I've got to find out if Sebastian is here. The best way to do that seems to be sticking close to ben Hashir."

"Just watch out for yourself," Honey advised. "I've got it on good authority that that man has more hands than an octopus."

Mollie managed to laugh, though she was feeling anything but amused. Her survey of the crowded room turned up no sign of Sebastian, yet according to Messenger he should have arrived by now. She could only hope that he was somewhere else in the apartment, and that she would be able to find him.

"Ah, there you are," a voice at her elbow said. She turned to find her host smiling at her admiringly. Tex and Honey had drifted away, so they were as alone as anyone could possibly be in such a crowd.

"I've decided that my duties are over for the evening," ben Hashir said, "and I am free to devote myself to the loveliest of my guests."

"Why how charming of you," Mollie said, wincing inwardly. "That is, if you mean me." She swallowed her distaste and gave him a warm smile.

"Who else could I possibly mean?" he asked, taking her arm and steering her toward a relatively quiet corner. "How is it that we haven't met before?"

"Oh, I've been out of the country. Traveling, you know. Paris, London, Rome, all those places. So interesting."

"But not the Arab countries? A pity, you would be very popular there."

"I don't think I could wear one of those—what do you call them?—*chaldors*. The black cover-up thing. I'd just positively melt in one of those."

"Then you would stay inside," ben Hashir said as he took a step closer. "In the home of whatever lucky man you happened to be visiting. Myself, perhaps. I will be returning to Libya soon and would be honored to receive a visit from you."

"How nice," Mollie murmured, wondering how much longer she was going to be able to keep him at arm's length. At the rate they were going, she would shortly be pressed up against the nearest wall with no further room for maneuvering.

"This is such a lovely apartment," Mollie said, her breathlessness not completely false. Ben Hashir was uncomfortably close. She could smell his aftershave and feel the heat of his body, not unpleasant in themselves, but definitely so in view of their connotations. In an effort to put some distance between them, she added, "I'd love to see the rest of it."

"My pleasure," he assured her. "I do have some rather nice antiques, if you don't mind my saying so. Are you interested in furnishings?" The look he shot her said that he suspected she was not, but that was fine with him, since he also had other pursuits in mind.

"Well, I certainly don't know as much about them as Momma does, but I can tell my Louis Quinze from my George Fourth. In fact, wasn't that a Georgian desk I glimpsed in the library?"

"You have looked in the library?"

"Just a peek, when you came out. It looked most impressive."

"Other rooms are more interesting. If you would allow me . . ."

The touch of his fingers on her arm made her want to recoil, but she held herself still and managed another smile. "Of course; lead the way."

Whatever he had in mind to show her was apparently on the other side of the apartment. She tried to come up with some plausible way of drawing him back toward the library, since she now believed that if Sebastian was anywhere in the apartment, he was there.

Ben Hashir's reluctance to show it to her convinced her of that.

But before she could even attempt to do so, the door to the library opened again and the object of her thoughts emerged. Her breath caught in her throat as she took in Sebastian's appearance. Elegantly dressed in a black dinner jacket and white silk shirt, he was the epitome of male grace and strength.

More than a few of the lovely women in the room turned to look at him, even as Mollie did. But she suspected that only she caught the quick look of shock and anger that darkened his features in the instant when he recognized her. It was gone in a moment, replaced by urbane impassivity, as he crossed the room to where she and ben Hashir were standing.

"I got tired of waiting," he told their host, who was frowning at him. Turning to Mollie, he added, "I don't believe we've had the pleasure."

Disengaging her arm from ben Hashir's hold, which had suddenly become unpleasantly tight, she said, "Sue Bendel, from Houston. And who might you be?"

"Sebastian Barnett. You're going to think me very rude, Miss Bendel, but Mr. ben Hashir and I were in the midst of a conversation that really needs to be concluded." Turning to the Libyan, he said, "May I suggest we return to the library and resume our talk?"

Before ben Hashir could respond, Mollie chimed in. "Why, Mr. Barnett, however can you think of business at such a time? The fireworks are due to start in just a few minutes, aren't they, Abdul?"

Perhaps it was the use of his first name, or the enchanting smile she gave him. Whichever, ben Hashir stiffened in his resolve to make short work of the distraction. "It will only take a few minutes, my dear, and then I will be free to concentrate on you. I'll have a word with my associate, Barnett, and meet you in the library."

When the other man had gone, Sebastian leaned closer to Mollie, smiled for the benefit of anyone who happened to be watching, and said, "What in hell are you doing here?"

"Bringing you a gift from your friend Messenger." Turning so that his body blocked hers from the sight of anyone else in the room, she carefully removed the pistol from her purse and pressed it into his hand. "He said you wouldn't be able to get a weapon in because they'd search you. But they could hardly search all the guests, so I brought it."

"As I see," he said, swiftly pocketing the gun. "Messenger is going to be very sorry that he involved you. When I get through with him, he'll—"

"Never mind about him. All he was thinking about was keeping you alive, a goal I happen to heartily agree with."

"I want you to leave here right now," Sebastian said, ignoring her comments. "Make some excuse to ben Hashir and walk out."

"How do you expect me to do that?" she muttered, all too mindful of the crowd surrounding them. "I had to convince him that I was interested to get him to show me around. I thought they might be holding you somewhere and . . ."

"And you were going to rescue me?" He left no doubt as to what he thought of that. "Damn Messenger! I'll never forgive him for this."

"Would you stop going on about him?" she demanded. "Figure out what to do about Abdul. He's coming back."

The dark figure of the Arab threading his way through the crowd toward them drew them both up short. Sebastian managed a gracious smile as ben Hashir joined them. "Such a shame about your headache, Miss Bendel. Probably the best thing you could do is go home to bed."

"Nonsense, Mr. Barnett," she said firmly. "I feel perfectly fine. Besides, I wouldn't dream of missing all the fun."

"I'm so glad to hear that, my dear," ben Hashir said. "It will take only a few minutes to conclude my business with Mr. Barnett. I'll look forward to watching the fireworks with you."

Mollie gave him yet another enchanting and very encouraging smile, ignoring Sebastian's glare as she did so. Not until both men disappeared into the library did she slump slightly and swallow the fear that threatened to overwhelm her.

Chapter 14

It is not the policy of the United States government," Sebastian said quietly, "to negotiate with terrorists."

"Very laudatory," ben Hashir said as he poured
himself a cognac. He had offered one to his guest, who
had turned it down. "But what has that to do with
this, which after all is a matter between legitimate
governments?"

"I'll let the legitimate part pass," Sebastian said. He
was leaning against the marble mantle in the library.
All around him, beautifully bound books in half a
dozen languages testified to his host's erudition.
Which proved nothing except that a good education
was no proof against treachery.

"Do I understand you to acknowledge that the document is in the possession of the Libyan government?" Sebastian asked with deceptive calm.

Ben Hashir was not misled. He shot him a chiding glance. "Surely you realize nothing is ever that simple. If this affair works out well, then, yes, the document was in the possession of my government. If it does not, then, no, we had nothing to do with it."

"Forgive me for appearing naive," Sebastian said. He came away from the mantle and studied the bindings of several books, his interest apparently absorbed by them. "You have an excellent library."

"Thank you," ben Hashir said with equal formality. "If we could return to the matter at hand..."

"The document. Where is it?"

"We can cover that later. First I must know what your government is willing to do."

"Surely my presence here is enough to indicate our sincerity?"

"Hardly. I will need something rather more substantial to take to the friends who trusted me with the document." Ben Hashir took a sip of his cognac and smiled faintly. "I'm sure you understand. My role in this is simply to assist both parties in bringing things to a happy conclusion."

"You must know that no one will believe that," Sebastian said. He had turned away from the books and was no longer pretending interest in anything except his host. "Your visa to enter the United States will certainly be revoked."

"A pity," ben Hashir said. "I will miss all this, but there are other places. London, Rome, Paris . . . Miss Bendel was just reminding me of how pleasant they can be."

If he expected Sebastian to rise to the bait, he was disappointed. Instead of reacting to the mention of Mollie, Sebastian said only, "I suppose anywhere will do, so long as you aren't required to return home." At ben Hashir's deliberately blank look, he laughed. "Adjusting to life in Mr. Qaddafi's Libya couldn't be very easy after what you've become accustomed to here."

Ben Hashir put down his glass and eyed his guest directly. "I am a good Arab, Mr. Barnett, and a good Moslem. Make no mistake about that. If you imagine my sympathies are at all divided, disabuse yourself of that notion at once."

"I had no such notion," Sebastian said smoothly. "I would never make the mistake of imagining you are anything other than what you are." The coldness of his tone made it clear what he considered that to be.

"Enough," ben Hashir said abruptly. "I have far better ways to spend my last few hours in this country than sparring with you. Again I put it to you, what is your government willing to do?"

"What it has to," Sebastian said, "but only if it is absolutely convinced that the document is actually in your possession."

"You can't possibly think we would come this far on a bluff?"

"Why not? It's been tried before. Besides, you must admit that this whole story is rather absurd."

"I admit nothing of the sort," ben Hashir shot back. "By this time you have undoubtedly seen the results of tests done on the document purporting to be the Declaration of Independence. You will know that it is a fake, and you will have searched the tunnel, hoping to find the original. But it is gone, Mr. Barnett; believe me when I tell you that. Neither you nor anyone else in your government will ever see it unless our demands are met."

At least he had dropped the pretense, Sebastian thought, and was no longer attempting to differentiate between the terrorists and the Libyan government. Their demands, and their goals, were one and the same.

"I can only repeat," Sebastian said smoothly, "what I told you at the beginning: the United States government does not negotiate with terrorists. We do not give in to blackmail."

"Then why are you here?" ben Hashir demanded angrily. "I know who you are, Mr. Barnett. I know about your organization. You are—what shall we say?—expediters, not diplomats."

"Expediters?" Sebastian repeated the word as though trying it on for size. "Yes, I like that. It's a fair description. All right, enough of the niceties. Let's get down to business. As I said, we won't negotiate, and we won't be blackmailed. However, that doesn't mean you and I can't reach some sort of accord."

"What do you have in mind?" ben Hashir asked suspiciously. He didn't like this hard, self-contained American. It was too difficult to read his thoughts and intentions. Doing his best to look unconcerned, he sat down on the couch and waited for Sebastian to take a seat facing him.

When he had done so, Sebastian said, "What I propose is a straight business deal. You have something I want to buy. We agree on a price, and you turn it over. Simple."

"Not exactly," ben Hashir said, feeling more confident. So the Americans were willing to trade after all. That would come as a nasty shock to their allies in the Middle East, who were counting on them to stand firm against the more radical elements. But then, he had always said the United States would ultimately prove to be weak.

"There's nothing complicated about it," Sebastian insisted. "We're willing to pay quite well for the real Declaration."

"Pay how? Not in dollars."

"Why not? The dollar has its ups and downs, but it's still a solid currency. Of course, if you'd prefer gold . . ."

"Guns," ben Hashir said flatly. "As well as the other weapons outlined in the original communiqué. Nothing else is acceptable."

"But with the money you could buy guns."

"Who from? The Russians? No thank you. Their influence is already too great. Besides, generally speaking, your armaments are superior."

"Thank you," Sebastian said gravely. "This does, however, present certain problems. The United States can hardly be seen engaging in an arms deal with Libya."

Since the outcry that would be sure to cause was exactly what ben Hashir and his superiors hoped to bring about, the Libyan could only smile. "I'm sure we can come to some accommodation," he said soothingly, thinking all the while of the headlines that would burst upon the world when this news came out.

"Perhaps a conduit of front men," Sebastian suggested thoughtfully. "There are always arms merchants willing to take a cut of a major deal in order to spare governments embarrassment."

"An excellent idea," ben Hashir said. He was feeling better by the moment. With luck he would be enjoying the charms of the lovely Miss Bendel before the evening was out.

"We can work out the technical details later," Sebastian was saying. "But first, I must see the document." When ben Hashir started to demur, he added firmly, "otherwise, we have absolutely nothing to discuss."

Reluctantly, the Libyan nodded. "All right, but I must point out to you that this apartment is filled with guards. Should you be so foolish as to attempt to leave with the document, you will be stopped instantly."

"Please don't insult my intelligence," Sebastian said. "I'm not interested in being either a martyr or a hero."

After a long, assessing look, ben Hashir decided that he believed him. The American appeared tough and uncompromising, not at all the sort of soft-headed idealist who might be tempted to do something foolish.

"All right," he said at length. "I will allow you to examine it, but then we come to terms. Understood?"

"Fine with me. The sooner we can wrap this up, the sooner I can get back to more important matters."

"You surprise me. Surely the protection of such a vital part of your national heritage is important?"

"It's only a piece of paper to me," Sebastian said, watching intently as ben Hashir got up and walked toward a painting on the opposite wall. He had spotted it earlier, noting that it was flush with the wall instead of hanging slightly away from it. As he had suspected, it was attached by hinges and opened to reveal a small safe.

"Something of a cliché, I admit," ben Hashir said with a shrug, "but still effective. Besides, it was never intended that the document should be here for very long."

"Wise of you to insist on that. I'm sure you won't be surprised to know that others in my government favored a different approach."

"What did they have in mind?" ben Hashir asked as he twirled the dial. "A sudden attack by Delta Force, or some equally dramatic, and foolhardy, gesture?"

"Something like that," Sebastian murmured. The safe door was swinging open. Ben Hashir stretched his hand into it and withdrew a roll of parchment tied with a frayed ribbon.

"Not very impressive-looking, is it?" the Libyan said as he handed it to Sebastian. "But then, as you said, it's only a piece of paper."

A piece of paper that held the heart and soul of a nation. Not that Sebastian saw any reason to mention that. He took the parchment as casually as he could and set it down on the table.

"Was it found like this?"

"Rolled? Yes, it was. Of course, we opened it to make sure of what we were dealing with, but rest assured that proper precautions were taken. We understood that if it was damaged, it would be of little use."

Sebastian was relieved to hear that. Carefully he untied the ribbon and laid it aside, trying not to think as he did so of the men who had given their lives to protect the document he was about to examine.

For more than a hundred and fifty years it had lain hidden in the tunnel until simple bad luck placed it in the hands of their enemies. For the sake of the men who had already died, and for the sake of all the generations that had come after them and were still to come, he had to succeed.

"The paper is very fragile," he said quietly as he unrolled it.

"Not surprising, considering its age. My experts tell me that it is in better condition than might otherwise be expected, thanks to the humidity in the tunnel that kept it from drying out."

He was right about that, at least. Sebastian was relieved to see how well the document took to being unrolled. Only a few tiny pieces frayed away; otherwise it emerged intact.

Quickly he scanned it, taking in as he did the familiar words:

> We hold these truths to be self-evident, that all men are created equal, that they are endowed by their Creator with certain unalienable Rights, that among these are Life, Liberty and the pursuit of Happiness. That to secure these rights, Governments are instituted among Men, deriving their just powers from the consent of the governed . . .

And so on down through the listings of wrongs done to a proud people and their attempts to right them, until he came to the end:

> We, therefore, the Representatives of the United States of America, in General Congress, Assembled . . . do . . . solemnly publish and declare, That these United Colonies are, and of Right ought to be Free and Independent States . . . And for the

support of this Declaration, with a firm reliance on the Protection of Divine Providence, we mutually pledge to each other our Lives our Fortunes and our sacred Honor.

"It looks like the real thing to me," Sebastian said as he straightened slowly. He took a deep breath, fighting to regain the air of unconcern he knew he must continue to project if he was to have any chance of succeeding.

"Of course it is," ben Hashir said as Sebastian carefully re-rolled the document and fastened the ribbon around it once again. "Do you really think we would have gone to such lengths for a forgery?"

"Stranger things have happened," Sebastian murmured. He had the document in one hand and was reaching inside his coat pocket with the other. "For example, a situation that seems to be in perfect control can suddenly turn out to be anything but."

"What are you talking about?" ben Hashir asked, suddenly uneasy. He didn't like the unholy glint in the American's eyes, or the growing suspicion that he might somehow have misjudged him.

"We're going for a walk," Sebastian said easily, pointing the gun Mollie had given him directly at ben Hashir's heart. "You're going to do your best to see that I get out of here safely. Remember," he smiled faintly, "it isn't smart to be either a hero or a martyr."

His host's gaze was riveted on the pistol. "How did you get that? You were searched."

"Never mind. Let's get going." He gestured with the gun toward the door. "I don't want to panic your guests, so we'll walk very close together. Believe me when I say that at the first sign of trouble, I'll fire."

Ben Hashir did believe him; he had no choice when faced with such implacable determination. Though he raged inwardly, he nodded and said, "Don't do anything foolish. I'm no more eager to die than you are."

"Then we shouldn't have any problem." At the door, he paused long enough to adjust the document more firmly under his arm and press the gun against the small of ben Hashir's back. "Let's see how good an actor you are. We're two business associates who have just concluded a mutually successful deal. You couldn't be happier."

Ben Hashir shot him a venomous look and tried to smile, without much success. They left the library and headed into the crowd of guests, who were beginning to congregate near the windows. It wouldn't be long now before the fireworks started.

Sebastian caught sight of Mollie standing nearby. Her face was white and strained, but her eyes lit up when she saw him. He cocked his head toward the door. She understood and began heading in that direction.

"So the lovely Miss Bendel was in on this," ben Hashir said. "A pity. I would have enjoyed getting to know her better."

"Keep moving," Sebastian ordered. He would not allow himself to entertain any thoughts of Mollie with the Libyan, not when any distraction could prove fatal for both her and himself.

A large, blank-faced man standing near the door abruptly straightened when he caught sight of his employer and the American. He started to take a step forward, only to be stopped by a curt gesture from ben Hashir.

"Smart," Sebastian said in his ear. "Keep your goons well away from me, otherwise anything might happen."

Another of the guards had spotted them and started forward, only to be stopped by the Libyan. They were almost at the door when Mollie joined them. "Have you got it?" she asked softly.

Sebastian nodded. "Under my arm. Take it." When she hesitated, he added, "I wouldn't want anything to spoil my aim."

She did as he said, cradling the parchment roll against her. It felt so light and fragile that she was almost afraid to touch it.

"We'll go through the door and down the corridor to the elevators," Sebastian was saying. "Our friend here," he gestured at ben Hashir, "will stay with us every step of the way."

"When will you release me?" the Libyan demanded. "I've done nothing wrong. You can't even claim that the Declaration was stolen, since you didn't know where it was until we brought it to your attention."

"For which I'm sure we'll always be grateful," Sebastian said coldly. "I'll let you go when I'm sure it's safe, not before."

"I don't believe you. You have no intention of releasing me. I'll be a hostage myself."

"Calm down," Sebastian ordered, concerned by the rising note of hysteria in the other man's voice. "Just consider this a little experience in how the other side feels. Next time somebody talks about taking hostages, maybe you won't think it's such a hot idea."

Ben Hashir gave no sign of hearing him. His face was flushed, and his eyes were wide with terror. Sebastian couldn't really blame him for being afraid. Whatever happened, the Libyan was in big trouble. Either he would end up a prisoner of the Americans, or be shipped home for failing to carry out his mission. On balance, an American jail might look pretty good.

Ben Hashir, however, apparently didn't think so. They were about to start down the corridor leading to the door when he suddenly let out a strangled scream and darted to one side.

As he did so, he reached out and yanked Mollie with him, pulling her into Sebastian's line of fire. Only years of rigorous training and discipline prevented Sebastian from shooting. As it was, he had only a split second in which he managed to wrest her from the Libyan's grasp before the guards would reach them.

Ben Hashir had fled down the hallway toward the library. The guards were closing in fast. Sebastian knew that their route to the door was sealed off, and they were within seconds of capture when he spotted the windows.

"Come on," he said, pulling Mollie after him. They fought their way through the crowd of guests, still happily oblivious to what was going on, and reached the window. It opened onto a terrace, beyond which lay only darkness.

Orange trees in wooden buckets were scattered over the terrace, their fragrance perfuming the humid night air. Rows of boxwood hedges outlined beds of flowering plants. Roses, tulips and lilies bloomed in profusion. Neat gravel paths wound between the flower beds, all aiming inward, like the spokes of a wheel, toward a gently bubbling fountain.

Mollie had heard that such fantasies as formal English gardens existed high above the streets of Manhattan, but she had never seen such a thing before. Momentarily taken aback, she stopped, only to be yanked back to reality by Sebastian.

"They're right behind us. Keep going."

As she obeyed, she dared a glance over her shoulder. The guards were hard on their heels, and in the moonlight she could see the metallic glint of the weapons they carried.

"Wh-where," she gasped, "are we going?"

"I don't know," Sebastian admitted reluctantly. They had come to the edge of the terrace. Nothing stood between them and empty air except a waist-high stone wall. Mollie looked down some twenty stories to the ground below and felt her senses reel.

Sebastian saw her dismay and tightened his hold on her waist. "Over there," he said, urging her toward the side of the building. Another apartment house had been built flush up against it. There was no space between them, but the roof lines did not meet; the other building was about fifteen feet lower in height.

"We'll have to climb down," Sebastian said as he quickly scanned the wall. "Lucky it's an old building. The stones should provide plenty of holds."

"For you, maybe," Mollie gasped. "Not for me. I've never done any climbing."

"Kick off your shoes," he instructed, choosing to ignore her protest. "You're about to get a crash course." As he spoke, the guards opened fire. They had held off until then to keep the guests from realizing what was happening, but seeing their quarry about to escape to the next roof, they had delayed no longer.

The first shot whizzed past Sebastian's head, making almost no sound, thanks to a silencer. He ducked, and pulled Mollie behind a wooden gardening shed. "There's no time to waste. I'll start and you follow. Put your feet and hands where I tell you. All right?"

She nodded mutely, only then realizing that she was still carrying the document. Quickly she lifted her skirt and placed it underneath, pulling it up under her waistband.

Sebastian gave her a quick, reassuring smile before starting down the wall. He moved with the litheness of a cat, his lean, taut body flowing easily over the stones. Mollie was considerably less confident. Her breath was in her throat as she gingerly lowered herself down the wall, clinging to it with fingers and toes. It was cold and hard against her, and the holds seemed impossibly narrow.

"You're doing fine," Sebastian called from directly below her. Move your left foot straight down to the next stone; then follow with your right."

She did as he said, and gasped with relief when her toes found the next tiny ledge. In the next instant the gasp turned to a moan of dismay as she heard Sebastian let go and drop to the roof.

"It's okay," he called as he came swiftly out of the crouch in which he had landed. "You're far enough down now, honey. Let go and I'll catch you."

Let go? She had just figured out how to hold on; moreover she was still eight feet off the ground. That might not have seemed such a terrifying distance under other circumstances, but as it was, it could have been miles.

"I can't," she whispered, hardly able to speak. Her fingers were digging into the stone, so tightly clenched that she truly believed she would not be able to release them.

"You've got to. The guards . . ."

He didn't have to finish. She could hear the running footsteps, knew that the guards would be literally on top of them at any moment. Taking a deep breath, she closed her eyes, thought of Sebastian and let herself fall.

He caught her before she could hit the roof, and set her gently on her feet. Around them the moonlight revealed another garden, less formal than the other, but no less beautiful. Its loveliness mocked them as they raced across it, all too aware that the guards were following the same route down and would quickly be within shooting range again.

On the chance that it might be open, Sebastian paused long enough to try the door to the stairs. When it failed to yield, he wasted no time on regrets but moved on. The next building was of almost the same height as the one they stood on, but this time there was an air space between them, perhaps six feet wide.

"We can jump it," he said confidently, though he felt anything but. He could make it easily, but Mollie was shorter than he and unaccustomed to such activity. She would have a much tougher time.

"I'll go first," he said, giving her no chance to object. He backed up far enough to get a running start, took several long strides, and hurled himself across the distance, clearing it easily.

When he looked back, Mollie stood with her hand over her mouth, her eyes wide and dark with terror that he somehow sensed was not for herself.

"See," he said quickly, "it's easy. Hoist up that long skirt and just start to run. I'll be right here to catch you."

She hesitated barely an instant before accepting that she had no choice. The guards were once again closing in. Shots winged past her; at any moment one of them would find its mark.

Taking a deep breath, she ran. At the edge of the roof, as her feet encountered only empty air, a scream bubbled up in her throat. She reached, straining, for the other side, only to know with sickening certainty that she had fallen short.

Everything seemed to be happening in slow motion. She saw the edge of the other roof and instinctively grasped at it. Her fingers brushed stone, then locked on it with a death grip as the rest of her body dangled into space.

Pain lanced through her arms as they took her entire weight. Immediately her fingers began to go numb. Sickening terror twisted her stomach. Desperately she resisted the impulse to look down, knowing that if she did so, she would be doomed.

Time seemed to stretch out through eternity, but in fact only seconds passed before Sebastian's arms lashed out. He seized hold of both her wrists, his steely strength taking her weight easily.

"It's all right," he said softly, though his taut face above her belied his seeming calm. "I've got you."

He began pulling her up, inch by inch, trying not to scrape her body against the rough stones. Mollie kept her eyes riveted on him, as if their locked gazes were a lifeline. When at last her feet touched the roof, she sobbed in relief and all but collapsed in his arms. He held her tightly to him, his face buried in her scented hair, and murmured her name over and over.

Until sound suddenly exploded all around them and the sky was lit with fire.

Chapter 15

Wh-what?" Mollie gasped, dazed by the sudden explosion that turned the night sky to burning reds and oranges.

"The fireworks," Sebastian said. "They've started."

A spinning catherine wheel orbited above them, followed swiftly by a volley of split comets in brilliant yellows and greens. A bursting shell spilled a cascade of glittering diamonds as another exploded outward into a burning flower.

All around them, from roof tops and windows, they could hear the cheers of the spectators. Still holding Mollie tightly against him, Sebastian slowly became aware that they were not alone. The guards had caught up with them and were standing directly on the other side of the air shaft. Their guns were raised, ready to shoot, but the sudden illumination of the fireworks had stripped away the veil of darkness.

Even as one of the men took aim, their leader snarled an order. Off to the side, another penthouse opened onto the terrace where Mollie and Sebastian stood. A startled woman could be seen behind a window, her mouth open and her hand pointing, not in pleasure, but in shock and fear. Already others had begun to gather behind her, the fireworks forgotten as they stared at the deadly panorama being played out before them.

The rockets continued to burst, sending shards of brilliantly colored light through the sky. Far below, on the darkened street, the wail of police sirens began as a faint cry in the distance and swiftly grew to a crescendo.

Mollie heard none of it. Nestled against Sebastian, she knew only that they had stopped running and that no one was shooting at them. Soon there were people crowding around, asking questions, but she ignored them.

Not until they were seated inside a strange apartment and a young woman in a uniform was bending over her, asking if she needed a doctor, did she emerge from the cocoon of numbness.

"Doctor? No, I'm fine. Where . . . where is Sebastian?"

"The man you were with? He's talking with the police. Everything's all right now," the young woman added gently. "You're safe."

Mollie nodded absently and got to her feet. She swayed slightly, but the policewoman kept her from falling. Swiftly regaining her balance, Mollie managed a smile. "I guess we took everyone by surprise."

The woman grinned. "You could say that again. This is a Fourth of July none of those people out there will ever forget. Say, would you mind telling me what was going on?"

"It's a long story," Mollie murmured, becoming aware of something uncomfortable pressing into her stomach. She put a hand against her dress and heard the rustle of parchment.

Remembrance flooded back. Swiftly she lifted her skirt and removed the rolled document. "What's that?" the policewoman asked, staring at it curiously.

"Just an old piece of paper," Mollie said quietly. She held it between her hands, really seeing it for the first time since she had taken it from Sebastian. Considering everything it had been through, especially recently, it appeared to be in quite good condition.

Greatly relieved that she had done it no harm, she held on to it carefully as she left the room and, followed by the policewoman, went in search of Sebastian.

It wasn't difficult to find him. The owners of the penthouse had graciously turned their living room

over to the authorities, who were busy taking state-
ments. Sebastian sat off to one side, looking completely unruffled as he chatted with a tall man in a
business suit. When he caught sight of Mollie, he
smiled and held out a hand.

"This is Lieutenant Lancaster of the New York Police Department. He's smoothing all this out for us."

Mollie wasn't quite sure what that meant, but she
nodded politely to the detective, who was looking at
her intently. "Nice to meet you, ma'am," he said.
"We'll wrap this up as quietly as possible; the organization won't be mentioned, of course. Mr. Barnett
has given me all the information I need, so you're both
free to go whenever you like."

She nodded pleasantly, pretending that she understood what he was saying, but the moment she was
alone with Sebastian, her curiosity could no longer be
contained.

"What did you tell him?" she asked as they walked
down the corridor toward the elevators. "How come
he's letting us go so easily? Did they capture ben
Hashir's goons, not to mention ben Hashir?"

"One question at a time," Sebastian pleaded,
laughing. He waited until they were in the elevator,
then turned to her and drew her into his arms. "And
first, before I answer any of them, I want to be sure
you're really all right."

The kiss they shared, long and passionate, must
have convinced him. Certainly he looked properly
impressed when he finally raised his head to discover

that they had arrived at the lobby and were being viewed by an indulgent couple waiting for the elevator.

"Isn't that sweet, John?" they heard the woman say as they hurriedly exited. "Young people still fall in love."

"Always did, Martha," he replied tenderly. "Always did."

"You're not going to distract me like that," Mollie insisted, somewhat breathlessly. "I want to know what happened."

"Fair enough. Your friends, Tex and Honey Bendel, saw our little altercation with ben Hashir and got on the phone to the number they'd been given in case of an emergency. They reached Messenger, who called in the police. We have a working relationship with all police departments; they assist us as needed and keep attention off the organization."

"How convenient," she murmured. "So ben Hashir and the guards were caught?"

"All neatly tied up in a net that not even they can get out of. The charges against them are pretty stiff—attempted murder, attempted kidnapping, assault with a deadly weapon, and so on. Odds are they'll cooperate in return for reduced sentences, not that they won't still be spending a considerable length of time in prison."

He smiled faintly as they strolled across the street. "Actually, they might prefer that. Having screwed up

as thoroughly as they did, life on the outside might not
be too healthy for a while.''

Mollie really couldn't have cared less what happened to the Libyans, so long as they were in custody.
It was beginning to get through to her that Sebastian's mission was all but completed. The purpose that
had brought them together in the first place was almost ended.

More than anything, she wanted to ask him what
would happen now. But the words caught in her
throat, and at any rate, she had no opportunity, since
a big, black car had suddenly pulled up in front of
them.

''I thought he'd be around here somewhere,'' Sebastian muttered. He stood perfectly still, his arm
around Mollie, as Messenger got out of the back seat.

The older man approached them somewhat hesitantly, clearly wary of what his reception would be. He
needn't have wondered; Sebastian wasted no time setting him straight.

''You bastard,'' he said with implacable firmness.
''What the hell were you thinking of to send Mollie in
there?''

''Of you,'' Messenger replied, flinching only
slightly, ''and of that.'' He gestured toward the
parchment roll she still clutched. ''I see you got it
out.''

''And risked her life in the process,'' Sebastian
snarled. He was beyond anger, beyond relief that the

mission had succeeded, beyond anything except the sheer, gut-wrenching fear that Mollie might have died.

Then another thought occurred to him, and he smiled faintly. So this was love, this all-encompassing exaltation, this half-terrifying, half-thrilling sense of no longer being alone, of being part of another person whose life he valued to be every bit as great as his own. No wonder poets claimed it drove men mad.

Messenger saw the change in him and was briefly puzzled, until he recognized the tender look that lit the gray eyes gazing at Mollie. Once, long ago, in what seemed like another life, he had also known love. His had been lost, to his everlasting regret, but he could still rejoice to know that such was not always the case.

"So you've finally fallen, old boy?" he said with a grin. "Happens to the best of us, though I must admit I hate to lose my top agent."

Mollie looked from one to the other of them in bewilderment. They seemed to be speaking in some sort of code beyond her grasp. Or was it merely the shorthand of men who understood each other? All she was really sure of was that Messenger had said something about losing Sebastian. She hardly dared to believe what that seemed to mean.

"We'll be in touch," Sebastian was saying as he gently took the rolled parchment from Mollie and handed it to the older man. "Give Alpha my regards."

"I'm sure you'll be hearing from him," Messenger said. The President wasn't going to be any too pleased, either, when he heard about Eagle's leaving. At least the recovery of the Declaration should soothe him.

"What will they do with it?" Mollie asked as they strolled down the block toward where Sebastian had left his car.

"Switch it with the fake that's been on display all this time," he said. "It will be done very quietly, of course. To do otherwise would be to invite all sorts of questions better left unasked for the moment.

"But someday," he added, as he unlocked the car door and helped her in, "the truth will come out. In calmer times, when the problems we face right now have been solved."

"Do you really believe they will be?" she asked. He had slid behind the wheel and started the Jaguar. It moved smoothly down the almost deserted street. The fireworks had ended, and the crowds had gone home, no one among them suspecting what that night had brought.

"I have to believe it," Sebastian said quietly. "After all, that's what I've worked for all these years. It's hard to see when you're so close to a situation, but we are making progress. Slowly, perhaps, but progress all the same.

"What Messenger said about losing you, what did he mean?"

He cast her a quick look. "Isn't it obvious? I'm resigning."

Mollie took a deep breath, trying to still the sudden, almost painful racing of her heart. "Why?

You've been in it so many years, why suddenly decide to give it up?"

"Because," he said very quietly, "I've found something that's more important to me." When she didn't respond, mainly because she couldn't, he went on. "Back there on that rooftop, when you almost fell, I realized what it would mean to lose someone you love. I can't put you through that, always wondering what is going to happen to me.

"Besides," he added, "I'm tired of living that way myself. I want something different, better. The kind of life we shared in Connecticut."

"That was very brief," Mollie pointed out, forcing herself to be at least a little reasonable. It wasn't easy. Inside she was close to exploding with joy, not unlike the glowing fireworks that had lately lit the sky. Yet she felt constrained to point out, "We don't really know each other all that well."

"I know you better than I've ever known anyone besides myself," he said quietly. "And I know what you mean to me."

Faced with such honesty, Mollie could not help but respond in kind. "I love you, Sebastian," she said gently. "That's the first time I've said that to a man."

"You picked a hell of a place to do it," he said with a slightly shaky laugh. "Where I can't show you how it makes me feel."

"We aren't far from your place, are we?"

"No," he agreed, stepping down slightly on the accelerator. "Will Mehitabel forgive us for leaving her alone tonight?"

"I think she'll overlook it," Mollie said, "in view of her obvious fondness of you."

"I'll make it up to her," he promised. "She'll have her weight in tuna fish."

She laughed softly. "You certainly know the way to a girl's heart."

"Actually, for you I had something different in mind—a ring, a white dress, a honeymoon. How does that sound?"

"Like my mother will be in heaven," she murmured. "I hope you realize what you're getting into."

He laughed as they turned into the garage under his building. "I think I've got a pretty fair idea, but just in case I've missed anything, perhaps you'd like to show me."

"Not here," Mollie said with her best New England primness.

Sebastian shot her a fetching leer. "Upstairs."

"Race you to the elevator."

In fact, they made it together, found the ride all too short, and stumbled out at his floor breathless and laughing.

After he had unlocked the door, Sebastian picked her up with a flourish and carried her inside. Setting her gently on her feet, he drew her to him. "I'm going to enjoy getting to know you better, Mollie Fletcher Barnett. Every lovely, enticing inch of you."

"And my mind, too," she said, unable to stop her giggling. "Don't forget about my mind."

"That's what first attracted me to you," he claimed loftily with a fine disregard for the facts. "I was fascinated to discover what sort of woman would be wandering around in a dank old tunnel at night."

"You thought I was a terrorist," she reminded him gently, only to be thoroughly distracted as he unzipped her dress.

"Where did you get this thing, anyway?"

"M-messenger, he wanted me to look the part."

"Mmmm, maybe he's not so bad after all."

"Does he really believe you've quit?" she asked suddenly as cool air touched her bare skin.

"He'd better, because I have. From now on it's just plain old Barnett, husband and teacher."

He really believed it, she realized, and allowed herself to wonder for just a moment if he would be satisfied with that.

Then all thought fled as his hands and lips began to work their magic on her body. Far off in the sky, one last, lone rocket soared, exploding in a radiant shower of gold. Its light shone a benediction on the man and woman entwined in love.

Silhouette Intimate Moments

COMING
NEXT MONTH

MAN FOR HIRE—Parris Afton Bonds
Alyx needed to hire a man to help her rescue her
kidnapped daughter. Khalid Rajhi was a desert sheikh
who gave not only his help, but his heart.

THE OLD FLAME—Alexandra Sellers
Sondra had always recognized the power Ben held
over her, and never more clearly than now, when there
seemed no way to escape him, on the job or off.

SWEET REASON—Sandy Steen
Laine had no intention of falling in love while on
vacation in Mexico, much less getting involved with a
case of espionage. But Drew Kenyon had a way of
blowing intentions and expectations to the wind.

WHEN WE TOUCH—Mary Lynn Baxter
The FBI wanted Blair Browning back, and they knew
just how to get her. Caleb Hunt wanted Blair, too, for
a very personal reason—and he, too, seemed destined
for success.

A terrible family secret drives Kristi Johannssen to
California, where she finds glamor, romance
and...a threat to her life!

BEYOND
THE
RAINBOW

MARGARET CHITTENDEN

Power and elegance, jealousy and deceit, even murder, stoke
fires of passion in this glittering novel set in the fashion world
of Hollywood, on the dazzling coast of Southern California.

FOUR UNIQUE SERIES
FOR EVERY WOMAN YOU ARE...

Silhouette Romance

Heartwarming romances that will make you
laugh and cry as they bring you all the wonder
and magic of falling in love.

6 titles
per month

Silhouette Special Edition

Expanded romances written with emotion and
heightened romantic tension to ensure
powerful stories. A rare blend of passion and
dramatic realism.

6 titles
per month

Silhouette Desire

Believable, sensuous, compelling—and
above all, romantic—these stories deliver
the promise of love, the guarantee
of satisfaction.

6 titles
per month

Silhouette Intimate Moments

Love stories that entice; longer, more
sensuous romances filled with adventure,
suspense, glamour and melodrama.

4 titles
per month